Joseph Conrad by Hugh Walpole

Sir Hugh Seymour Walpole, CBE was born in Auckland, New Zealand, on March 13th, 1884.

His parents had moved to New Zealand in 1877, but his mother, Mildred, unable to settle there, eventually persuaded her husband, Somerset, an Anglican clergyman, to accept another post, this time in New York in 1889. Walpole's early years involved being educated by a Governess until, in 1893, his parents decided he needed an English education and the young Walpole was sent to England.

He first attended a preparatory school in Truro. He naturally missed his family but was reasonably happy. A move to Sir William Borlase's Grammar School in Marlow in 1895, found him bullied, frightened and miserable.

The following year, 1897, the Walpole's returned to England and Walpole was moved to be a day boy at Durham School. His sense of isolation increased. His refuge was the local library and reading.

From 1903 to 1906 Walpole studied history at Emmanuel College, Cambridge and there, in 1905, had his first work published, the critical essay "Two Meredithian Heroes".

Walpole was also attempting to cope with and come to terms with his homosexual feelings and to find "that perfect friend".

After a short spell tutoring in Germany and then teaching French at Epsom in 1908 he found the desire to fully immerse himself in the literary world. He moved to London to become a book reviewer for The Standard and to write fiction in his spare time. In 1909, he published his first novel, The Wooden Horse. The book received good reviews but sold little.

Better was to come in 1911 when he published Mr Perrin and Mr Traill. In early 1914 Henry James wrote an article for The Times Literary Supplement surveying the younger generation of British novelists. Walpole was greatly encouraged that one of the greatest living authors had publicly ranked him among the finest young British novelists.

As war approached, Walpole realised that his poor eyesight would disqualify him from service and accepted an appointment, based in Moscow, reporting for The Saturday Review and The Daily Mail. Although allowed to visit the front in Poland, these dispatches were not enough to stop hostile comments at home that he was not 'doing his bit' for the war effort.

Walpole was ready with a counter; an appointment as a Russian officer, in the Sanitar. He explained they were "part of the Red Cross that does the rough work at the front, carrying men out of the trenches, helping at the base hospitals in every sort of way, doing every kind of rough job".

During a skirmish in June 1915 Walpole rescued a wounded soldier; his Russian comrades refused to help and this meant Walpole had to carry one end of a stretcher, dragging the man to safety. He was awarded the Cross of Saint George. By late 1917 it was clear to Walpole, and the authorities, that his work was at an end. In London Walpole joined the Foreign Office and remained there until resigning in February 1919. For his wartime work he was awarded the CBE in 1918.

Walpole continued to write and publish and now also began a career on the highly lucrative lecture tour in the United States.

In 1924 Walpole moved to a house, Brackenburn, near Keswick in the Lake District. Although he maintained a flat in Piccadilly, Brackenburn was to be his main home for the rest of his life.

At the end of 1924 Walpole met Harold Cheevers, who soon became his friend and constant companion and remained so for the rest of his life; "that perfect friend".

Hollywood, in the shape of MGM, invited him in 1934 to write the script for a film of David Copperfield. He also had a small acting role in the film.

In 1937 Walpole was offered a knighthood. He accepted although Kipling, Hardy, Galsworthy had all refused. "I'm not of their class... Besides I shall like being a knight," he said.

Unfortunately his health was undermined by diabetes made worse by the frenetic pace of his life. Sir Hugh Seymour Walpole, CBE died of a heart attack at Brackenburn, aged 57 on June 1st, 1941. He was buried in St John's churchyard in Keswick.

Index of Contents
CHAPTER I - Biography
CHAPTER II - The Novelist
CHAPTER III - The Poet
CHAPTER IV - Romance and Realism
HUGH WALPOLE – A SHORT BIOGRAPHY
HUGH WALPOLE – A CONCISE BIBLIOGRAPHY

CHAPTER I

BIOGRAPHY

I

To any reader of the books of Joseph Conrad it must be at once plain that his immediate experiences and impressions of life have gone very directly to the making of his art. It may happen often enough that an author's artistic life is of no importance to the critic and that his dealing with it is merely a personal impertinence and curiosity, but with the life of Joseph Conrad the critic has something to do, because, again and again, this writer deliberately evokes the power of personal reminiscence, charging it with the burden of his philosophy and the creation of his characters.

With the details of his life we cannot, in any way, be concerned, but with the three backgrounds against whose form and colour his art has been placed we have some compulsory connection.

Joseph Conrad (Teodor Josef Konrad Karzeniowski) was born on 6th December 1857, and his birthplace was the Ukraine in the south of Poland. In 1862 his father, who had been concerned in the last Polish rebellion, was banished to Vologda. The boy lived with his mother and father there until his mother died, when he was sent back to the Ukraine. In 1870 his father died.

Conrad was then sent to school in Cracow and there he remained until 1874, when, following an absolutely compelling impulse, he went to sea. In the month of May, 1878, he first landed on English ground; he knew at that time no English but learnt rapidly, and in the autumn of 1878 joined the Duke of Sutherland as ordinary seaman. He became a Master in the English Merchant Service in 1884, in which year he was naturalised. In 1894 he left the sea, whose servant he had been for nearly twenty years: he sent the manuscript of a novel that he had been writing at various periods during his sea life to Mr Fisher Unwin. With that publisher's acceptance of Almayer's Folly the third period of his life began. Since then his history has been the history of his books.

Looking for an instant at the dramatic contrast and almost ironical relationship of these three backgrounds—Poland, the Sea, the inner security and tradition of an English country-side—one can realise what they may make of an artist. That early Polish atmosphere, viewed through all the deep light and high shade of a remembered childhood, may be enough to give life and vigour to any poet's temperament. The romantic melancholy born of early years in such an atmosphere might well plant deeply in any soul the ironic contemplation of an impossible freedom.

Growing into youth in a land whose farthest bounds were held by unlawful tyranny, Conrad may well have contemplated the sea as the one unlimited monarchy of freedom and, even although he were too young to realise what impulses those were that drove him, he may have felt that space and size and the force of a power stronger than man were the only conditions of possible liberty. He sought those conditions, found them and clung to them; he found, too, an ironic pity for men who could still live slaves and prisoners to other men when to them also such freedom was possible. That ironic pity he never afterwards lost, and the romance that was in him received a mighty impulse from that contrast that he was always now to contemplate. He discovered the Sea and paid to her at once his debt of gratitude and obedience. He thought it no hard thing to obey her when he might, at the same time, so honestly admire her and she has remained for him, as an artist, the only personality that he has been able wholeheartedly to admire. He found in her something stronger than man and he must have triumphed in the contemplation of the dominion that she could exercise, if she would, over the tyrannies that he had known in his childhood.

He found, too, in her service, the type of man who, most strongly, appealed to him. He had known a world composed of threats, fugitive rebellions, wild outbursts of defiance, inefficient struggles against tyranny. He was in the company now of those who realised so completely the relationship of themselves and their duty to their master and their service that there was simply nothing to be said about it. England had, perhaps, long ago called to him with her promise of freedom, and now on an English ship he realised the practice and performance of that freedom, indulged in, as it was, with the fewest possible words. Moreover, with his fund of romantic imagination, he must have been pleased by the contrast of his present company, men who, by sheer lack of imagination, ruled and served the most imaginative force in nature. The wonders of the sea, by day and by night, were unnoticed by his companions, and he admired their lack of vision. Too much vision had driven his country under the heel of Tyranny, had bred in himself a despair of any possible freedom for far-seeing men; now he was a citizen of a world where freedom reigned because men could not perceive how it could be otherwise; the two sides of the shield were revealed to him.

Then, towards the end of his twenty years' service of the sea, the creative impulse in him demanded an outlet. He wrote, at stray moments of opportunity during several years, a novel, wrote it for his pleasure and diversion, sent it finally to a publisher with all that lack of confidence in posts and publishers that every author, who cares for his creations, will feel to the end of his days. He has said that if Almayer's Folly had been refused he would never have written again, but we may well believe that, let the fate of that book be what it might, the energy and surprise of his discovery of the sea must have been declared to the world. Almayer's Folly, however, was not rejected; its publication caused The Spectator to remark: "The name of Mr Conrad is new to us, but it appears to us as if he might become the Kipling of the Malay Archipelago." He had, therefore, encouragement of the most dignified kind from the beginning. He himself, however, may have possibly regarded that day in 1897 when Henley accepted The Nigger of the Narcissus for The New Review as a more important date in his new career. That date may serve for the commencement of the third period of his adventure.

The quiet atmosphere of the England that he had adopted made the final, almost inevitable contrast with the earlier periods. With such a country behind him it was possible for him to contemplate in peace the whole "case" of his earlier life. It was as a "case" that he saw it, a "case" that was to produce all those other "cases" that were his books. This has been their history.

II

His books, also, find naturally a division into three parts; the first period, beginning with Almayer's Folly in 1895, ended with Lord Jim in 1900. The second contains the two volumes of Youth and Typhoon, the novel Romance that he wrote in collaboration with Ford Madox Hueffer, and ends with Nostromo, published in 1903. The third period begins, after a long pause, in 1907 with The Secret Agent, and receives its climax with the remarkable popularity of Chance in 1914, and Victory (1915).

His first period was a period of struggle, struggle with a foreign language, struggle with a technique that was always, from the point of view of the "schools," to remain too strong for him, struggles with the very force and power of his reminiscences that were urging themselves upon him, now at the moment of their contemplated freedom, like wild beasts behind iron bars. Almayer's Folly and The Outcast of the Islands (the first of these is sequel to the second) were remarkable in the freshness of their discovery of a new world. It was not that their world had not been found before, but rather that Conrad, by the force of his own individual discovery, proclaimed his find with a new voice and a new vigour. In the character of Almayer, of Aissa, of Willems, of Babalatchi and Abdulla there was a new psychology that gave promise of great things. Nevertheless these early stories were overcharged with atmosphere, were clumsy in their development and conveyed in their style a sense of rhetoric and lack of ease. His vision of his background was pulled out beyond its natural intensity and his own desire to make it overwhelming was so obvious as to frighten the creature into a determination to be, simply out of malicious perversity, anything else.

These two novels were followed by a volume of short stories, Tales of Unrest, that reveal, quite nakedly, Conrad's difficulties. One study in this book, The Return, with its redundancies and overemphasis, is the cruelest parody on its author and no single tale in the volume succeeds. It was, however, as though, with these efforts, Conrad flung himself free, for ever, from his apprenticeship; there appeared in 1898 what remains perhaps still his most perfect work, The Nigger of the Narcissus. This was a story entirely of the sea, of the voyage of a ship from port to port and of the influence upon that ship and upon the human souls that she contained, of the approaching shadow of death, an influence ironical, melancholy, never quite horrible, and always tender and humorous. Conrad must himself have loved, beyond all other vessels, the Narcissus. Never again, except perhaps in The Mirror of the Sea, was he to be so happily at his ease with any of his subjects. The book is a gallery of remarkably distinct and authentic portraits, the atmosphere is held in perfect restraint, and the overhanging theme is never, for an instant, abandoned. It is, above all, a record of lovingly cherished reminiscence. Of cherished reminiscence also was the book that closed the first period of his work, Lord Jim. This was to remain, until the publication of Chance, his most popular novel. It is the story of a young Englishman's loss of honour in a moment of panic and his victorious recovery. The first half of the book is a finely sustained development of a vividly remembered scene, the second half has the inevitability of a moral idea pursued to its romantic end rather than the inevitability of life. Here then in 1900 Conrad had worked himself free of the underground of the jungle and was able to choose his path. His choice was still dictated by the subjects that he remembered most vividly, but upon these rewards of observation his creative genius was working. James Wait, Donkin, Jim, Marlowe were men whom he had known, but men also to whom he had given a new birth.

There appeared now in Youth, Heart of Darkness and Typhoon three of the finest short stories in the English language, work of reminiscence, but glowing at its heart with all the lyrical exultation and flame of a passion that had been the ruling power of a life that was now to be abandoned. That salutation of farewell is in Youth and its evocation of the East, in The Heart of Darkness and its evocation of the forests that are beyond civilisation, in Typhoon and its evocation of the sea. He was never, after these tales, to write again of the sea as though he were still sailing on it. From this time he belonged, with regret and with some ironic contempt, to the land.

This second period closed with the production of a work that was deliberately created rather than reminiscent, Nostromo. Conrad may have known Dr Monyngham, Decoud, Mrs Gould, old Viola; but they became stronger than he and, in their completed personalities, owed no man anything for their creation. There is much to be said about Nostromo, in many ways the greatest of all Conrad's works, but, for the moment, one would only say that its appearance (it appeared first, of all ironical births, in a journal—T.P.'s Weekly—and astonished and bewildered its readers week by week, by its determination not to finish and yield place to something simpler) caused no comment whatever, that its critics did not understand it, and its author's own admirers were puzzled by its unlikeness to the earlier sea stories.

Nostromo was followed by a pause—one can easily imagine that its production did, for a moment, utterly exhaust its creator. When, however, in 1907 appeared The Secret Agent, a new attitude was most plainly visible. He was suddenly detached, writing now of "cases" that interested him as an investigator of human life, but called from his heart no burning participation of experience. He is tender towards Winnie Verloc and her old mother, the two women in The Secret Agent, but he studies them quite dispassionately. That love that clothed Jim so radiantly, that fierce contempt that in An Outcast of the Islands accompanied Willems to his degraded death, is gone. We have the finer artist, but we have lost something of that earlier compelling interest. The Secret Agent is a tale of secret service in London; it contains the wonderfully created figure of Verloc and it expresses, to the full, Conrad's hatred of those rows and rows of bricks and mortar that are so completely accepted by unimaginative men. In 1911 Under Western Eyes spoke strongly of a Russian influence. Turgéniev and Dostoievsky had too markedly their share in the creation of Razumov and the cosmopolitan circle in Geneva. Moreover, it is a book whose heart is cold.

A volume of short stories, A Set of Six, illustrating still more emphatically Conrad's new detachment, appeared in 1908 and is remarkable chiefly for an ironically humorous story of the Napoleonic wars—

The Duel—a tale too long, perhaps, but admirable for its sustained note. In 1912 he seemed, in another volume, 'Twixt Land and Sea, to unite some of his earlier glow with all his later mastery of his method. A Smile of Fortune and The Secret Sharer are amazing in the beauty of retrospect that they leave behind them in the soul of the reader. The sea is once more revealed to us, but it is revealed now as something that Conrad has conquered. His contact with the land has taken from him something of his earlier intimacy with his old mistress. Nevertheless The Secret Sharer is a most marvellous story, marvellous in its completeness of theme and treatment, marvellous in the contrast between the confined limitations of its stage and the vast implications of its moral idea. Finally in 1914 appeared Chance, by no means the finest of his books, but catching the attention and admiration of that wider audience who had remained indifferent to the force and beauty of The Nigger of the Narcissus, of Lord Jim, of Nostromo. With the popular success of Chance the first period of his work is closed. On the possible results of that popularity, their effect on the artist and on the whole world of men, one must offer, here at any rate, no prophecy.

III

To any reader who cares, seriously, to study the art of Joseph Conrad, no better advice could be offered than that he should begin with the reading of the two volumes that have been omitted from the preceding list. Some Reminiscences and The Mirror of the Sea demand consideration on the threshold of any survey of this author's work, because they reveal, from a personal, wilful and completely anarchistic angle, the individuality that can only be discovered, afterwards, objectively, in the process of creation.

In both these books Conrad is, quite simply, himself for anyone who cares to read. They are books dictated by no sense of precedent nor form nor fashion. They are books of their own kind, even more than are the novels. Some Reminiscences has only Tristram Shandy for its rival in the business of getting everything done without moving a step forward. The Mirror of the Sea has no rival at all.

We may suppose that the author did really intend to write his reminiscences when he began. He found a moment that would make a good starting-point, a moment in the writing of his first book, Almayer's Folly; at the conclusion or, more truly, cessation of Some Reminiscences, that moment is still hanging in mid-air, the writing of Almayer has not proceeded two lines farther down the stage, the maid-servant is still standing in the doorway, the hands of the clock have covered five minutes of the dial. What has occurred is simply that the fascination of the subject has been too strong. It is of the very essence of Conrad's art that one thing so powerfully suggests to him another that to start him on anything at all is a tragedy, because life is so short. His reminiscences would be easy enough to command would they only not take on a life of their own and shout at their unfortunate author: "Ah! yes. I'm interesting, of course, but don't you remember...?"

The whole adventure of writing his first book is crowded with incident, not because he considers it a wonderful book or himself a marvellous figure, but simply because any incident in the world must, in his eyes, be crowded about with other incidents. There is the pen one wrote the book with, that pen that belonged to poor old Captain B— of the Nonsuch who ... or there is the window just behind the writing-table that looked out into the river, that river that reminds one of the year '88 when ...

In the course of his thrilling voyage of discovery we are, by a kind of most blessed miracle, told something of Mr Nicholas B. and of the author's own most fascinating uncle. We even, by an extension of the miracle, learn something of Conrad as ship's officer (this the merest glimpse) and as a visitor to his uncle's house in Poland.

So by chance are these miraculous facts and glimpses that we catch at them with eager, extended hands, praying, imploring them to stay; indeed those glimpses may seem to us the more wonderful in that they have been, by us, only partially realised.

Nevertheless, in spite of its eager incoherence, at the same time both breathless, and, by the virtue of its author's style, solemn, we do obtain, in addition to our glimpses of Poland and the sea, one or two revelations of Conrad himself. Our revelations come to us partly through our impression of his own zest for life, a zest always ironical, often sceptical, but always eager and driven by a throbbing impulse of vitality. Partly also through certain deliberate utterances. He tells us:

"Those who read me know my conviction that the world, the temporal world, rests on a few very simple ideas; so simple that they must be as old as the hills. It rests, notably, amongst others, on the idea of Fidelity. At a time when nothing which is not revolutionary in some way or other can expect to attract much attention I have not been revolutionary in my writings." (Page 20.)

Or again:

"All claim to special righteousness awakens in me that scorn and anger from which a philosophical mind should be free." (Page 21.)

Or again:

"Even before the most seductive reveries I have remained mindful of that sobriety of interior life, that asceticism of sentiment, in which alone the naked form of truth, such as one conceives it, such as one feels it, can be rendered without shame." (Page 194.)

This simplicity, this fidelity, this hatred of self-assertion and self-satisfaction, this sobriety—these qualities do give some implication of the colour of the work that will arise from them; and when to these qualities we add that before-mentioned zest and vigour we must have some true conception of the nature of the work that he was to do.

It is for this that Some Reminiscences is valuable. To read it as a detached work, to expect from it the amiable facetiousness of a book of modern memories or the heavy authoritative coherence of the My Autobiography or My Life of some eminent scientist or theologian, is to be most grievously disappointed.

If the beginning is bewilderment the end is an impression of crowding, disordered life, of a tapestry richly dark, with figures woven into the very thread of it and yet starting to life with an individuality all their own. No book reveals more clearly the reasons both of Conrad's faults and of his merits. No book of his is more likely by reason of its honesty and simplicity to win him true friends. As a work of art there is almost everything to be said against it, except that it has that supreme gift that remains, at the end, almost all that we ask of any work of art, overwhelming vitality. But it is formless, ragged, incoherent, inconclusive, a fragment of eager, vivid, turbulent reminiscence poured into a friend's ear in a moment of sudden confidence. That may or may not be the best way to conduct reminiscences; the book remains a supremely intimate, engaging and enlightening introduction to its author.

With The Mirror of the Sea we are on very different ground. As I have already said, this is Conrad's happiest book—indeed, with the possible exception of The Nigger of the Narcissus, his only happy book. He is happy because he is able, for a moment, to forget his distrust, his dread, his inherent ironical pessimism. He is here permitting himself the whole range of his enthusiasm and admiration, and behind that enthusiasm there is a quiet, sure confidence that is strangely at variance with the distrust of his later novels.

The book seems at first sight to be a collection of almost haphazard papers, with such titles as Landfalls and Departures, Overdue and Missing, Rulers of East and West, The Nursery of the Craft. No reader however, can conclude it without having conveyed to him a strangely binding impression of Unity. He has been led, it will seem to him, into the very heart of the company of those who know the Sea as she really is, he has been made free of a great order.

The foundation of his intimacy springs from three sources—the majesty, power and cruelty of the Sea herself, the homely reality of the lives of the men who serve her, the vibrating, beautiful life of the ships that sail upon her. This is the Trilogy that holds in its hands the whole life and pageant of the sea; it is because Conrad holds all three elements in exact and perfect balance that this book has its unique value, its power both of realism, for this is the life of man, and of romance, which is the life of the sea.

Conrad's attitude to the Sea herself, in this book, is one of lyrical and passionate worship. He sees, with all the vivid accuracy of his realism, her deceits, her cruelties, her inhuman disregard of the lives of men, but, finally, her glory is enough for him. He will write of her like this:

"The sea—this truth must be confessed—has no generosity. No display of manly qualities—courage, hardihood, endurance, faithfulness—has ever been known to touch its irresponsible consciousness of power. The ocean has the conscienceless temper of a savage autocrat spoiled by much adulation. He cannot brook the slightest appearance of defiance, and has remained the irreconcilable enemy of ships and men ever since ships and men had the unheard-of audacity to go afloat together in the face of his frown ... the most amazing wonder of the deep is its unfathomable cruelty."

Nevertheless she holds him her most willing slave, and he is that because he believes that she alone in all the world is worthy to indulge this cruelty. She positively "brings it off," this assertion of her right, and once he is assured of that, he will yield absolute obedience. In this worship of the Sea and the winds that rouse her he allows himself a lyrical freedom that he was afterwards to check. He was never again, not even in Typhoon and Youth, to write with such free and spontaneous lyricism as in his famous passage about the "West Wind."

The Mirror of the Sea forms then the best possible introduction to Conrad's work, because it attests, more magnificently and more confidently than anything else that he has written, his faith and his devotion. It presents also, however, in its treatment of the second element of his subject, the men on the ships, many early sketches of the characters whom he, both before and afterwards, developed so fully in his novels. About these same men there are certain characteristics to be noticed, characteristics that must be treated more fully in a later analysis of Conrad's creative power, but that nevertheless demand some mention here as witnesses of the emotions, the humours, the passions that he, most naturally, observes. It is, in the first place, to be marked that almost all the men upon the sea, from "poor Captain B—, who used to suffer from sick headaches, in his young days, every time he was approaching a coast," to the dramatic Dominic ("from the slow, imperturbable gravity of that broad-chested man you would think he had never smiled in his life"), are silent and thoughtful. Granted this silence, Conrad in his half-mournful, half-humorous survey, is instantly attracted by any possible contrast. Captain B— dying in his home, with two grave, elderly women sitting beside him in the quiet room, "his eyes resting fondly upon the faces in the room, upon the pictures on the wall, upon all the familiar objects of that home whose abiding and clear image must have flashed often on his memory in times of stress and anxiety at sea"—"poor P—," with "his cheery temper, his admiration for the jokes in Punch, his little oddities—like his strange passion for borrowing looking-glasses, for instance"—that captain who "did everything with an air which put your attention on the alert and raised your expectations, but the result somehow was always on stereotyped lines, unsuggestive, empty of any lesson that one could lay to heart"—that other captain in whom "through a touch of self-seeking that modest artist of solid merit became untrue to his temperament"—here are little sketches for those portraits that afterwards we are to know so well, Marlowe, Captain McWhirr, Captain Lingard, Captain Mitchell and many others. Here we may fancy that his eye lingers as though in the mere enumeration of little oddities and contrasted qualities he sees such themes, such subjects, such "cases" that it is hard, almost beyond discipline, to leave them. Nevertheless they have to be left. He has obtained his broader contrast by his juxtaposition of the curious muddled jumble of the human life against the broad, august power of the Sea—that is all that his present subject demands, that is his theme and his picture.

Not all his theme, however; there remains the third element in it, the soul of the ship. It is, perhaps, after all, with the life of the ship that The Mirror of the Sea, ultimately, has most to do.

As other men write of the woman they have loved, so does Conrad write of his ships. He sees them, in this book that is so especially dedicated to their pride and beauty, coloured with a fine glow of romance, but nevertheless he realises them with all the accurate detail of a technician who describes his craft. You may learn of the raising and letting go of an anchor, and he will tell the journalists of their crime in speaking of "casting" an anchor when the true technicality is "brought up"—"to an anchor" understood. In the chapter on "Yachts" he provides as much technical detail as any book of instruction need demand and then suddenly there come these sentences—"the art of handling ships is finer, perhaps, than the art of handling men.".... "A ship is a creature which we have brought into the world, as it were on purpose to keep us up to mark."

Indeed it is the ship that gives that final impression of unity, of which I have already spoken, to the book. She grows, as it were, from her birth, in no ordered sequence of events, but admitting us ever more closely into her intimacy, telling us, at first shyly, afterwards more boldly, little things about herself, confiding to us her trials, appealing sometimes to our admiration, indulging sometimes our humour. Conrad is tender to her as he is to nothing human. He watches her shy, new, in the dock, "her reputation all to make yet in the talk of the seamen who were to share their life with her.".... "She looked modest to me. I imagined her diffident, lying very quiet, with her side nestling shyly against the wharf to which she was made fast with very new lines, intimidated by the company of her tried and experienced sisters already familiar with all the violences of the ocean and the exacting love of men."

Her friend stands there on the quay and bids her be of good courage; he salutes her grace and spirit—he echoes, with all the implied irony of contrast, his companion's "Ships are all right...."

He explains the many kinds of ships that there are—the rogues, the wickedly malicious, the sly, the benevolent, the proud, the adventurous, the staid, the decorous. For even the worst of these he has indulgences that he would never offer to the soul of man. He cannot be severe before such a world of fine spirits.

Finally, in the episode of the Tremolino and her tragic end (an end that has in it a suggestion of that later story, Freya of the Seven Islands), in that sinister adventure of Dominic and the vile Cæsar, he shows us, in miniature, what it is that he intends to do with all this material. He gives us the soul of the Tremolino, the soul of Dominic, the soul of the sea upon which they are voyaging. Without ever deserting the realism upon which he builds his foundations he raises upon it his house of romance.

This book remains by far the easiest, the kindest, the most friendly of all his books. He has been troubled here by no questions of form, of creation, of development, whether of character or of incident.

It is the best of all possible prologues to his more creative work.

CHAPTER II

THE NOVELIST

I

In discussing the art of any novelist as distinct from the poet or essayist there are three special questions that we may ask—as to the Theme, as to the Form, as to the creation of Character.

It is possible to discuss these three questions in terms that can be applied, in no fashion whatever, to the poem or the essay, although the novel may often more truly belong to the essay or the poem to the novel, as, for instance, The Ring and the Book and Aurora Leigh bear witness. All such questions of ultimate classes and divisions are vain, but these three divisions of Theme, Form and Character do cover many of the questions that are to be asked about any novelist simply in his position as novelist and nothing else. That Joseph Conrad is, in his art, most truly poet as well as novelist no reader of his work will deny. I wish, in this chapter, to consider him simply as a novelist—that is, as a narrator of the histories of certain human beings, with his attitude to those histories.

Concerning the form of the novel the English novelists, until the seventies and eighties of the nineteenth century, worried themselves but slightly. If they considered the matter they chuckled over their deliberate freedom, as did Sterne and Fielding. Scott considered story-telling a jolly business in which one was, also, happily able to make a fine living, but he never contemplated the matter with any respect. Jane Austen, who had as much form as any modern novelist, was quite unaware of her happy possession. The mid-Victorians gloriously abandoned themselves to the rich independence of shilling numbers, a fashion which forbade Form as completely as the manners of the time forbade frankness. A new period began at the end of the fifties; but no one in 1861 was aware that a novel called Evan Harrington was of any special importance; it made no more stir than did Almayer's Folly in the early nineties, although the wonderful Richard Feverel had already preceded it.

With the coming of George Meredith and Thomas Hardy the Form of the novel, springing straight from the shores of France, where Madame Bovary and Une Vie showed what might be done by taking trouble, grew into a question of considerable import. Robert Louis Stevenson showed how important it was to say things agreeably, even when you had not very much to say. Henry James showed that there was so much to say about everything that you could not possibly get to the end of it, and Rudyard

Kipling showed that the great thing was to see things as they were. At the beginning of the nineties everyone was immensely busied over the way that things were done. The Yellow Book sprang into a bright existence, flamed, and died. "Art for Art's sake" was slain by the trial of Oscar Wilde in 1895. Mr Wells, in addition to fantastic romances, wrote stories about shop assistants and knew something about biology. The Fabian Society made socialism entertaining. Mr Bernard Shaw foreshadowed a new period and the Boer War completed an old one.

Of the whole question of Conrad's place in the history of the English novel and his influence upon it I wish to speak in a later chapter. I would simply say here that if he was borne in upon the wind of the French influence he was himself, in later years, one of the chief agents in its destruction, but, beginning to write in English as he did in the time of The Yellow Book, passing through all the realistic reaction that followed the collapse of æstheticism, seeing the old period washed away by the storm of the Boer War, he had, especially prepared for him, a new stage upon which to labour. The time and the season were ideal for the work that he had to do.

II

The form in which Conrad has chosen to develop his narratives is the question which must always come first in any consideration of him as a novelist; the question of his form is the ground upon which he has been most frequently attacked.

His difficulties in this matter have all arisen, as I have already suggested, from his absorbing interest in life. Let us imagine, for an instant, an imaginary case. He has seen in some foreign port a quarrel between two seamen. One has "knifed" the other, and the quarrel has been watched, with complete indifference, by a young girl and a bibulous old wastrel who is obviously a relation both of hers and of the stricken seaman. The author sees here a case for his art and, wishing to give us the matter with the greatest possible truth and accuracy, he begins, oratio recta, by the narration of a little barber whose shop is just over the spot where the quarrel took place and whose lodgers the old man and the girl are. He describes the little barber and is, at once, amazed by the interesting facts that he discovers about the man. Seen standing in his doorway he is the most ordinary little figure, but once investigate his case and you find a strange contrast between his melancholy romanticism and the flashing fanaticism of his love for the young girl who lodges with him. That leads one back, through many years, to the moment of his first meeting with the bibulous old man, and for a witness of that we must hunt out a villainous old woman who keeps a drinking saloon in another part of the town. This old woman, now so drink-sodden and degraded, had once a history of her own. Once she was ...

And so the matter continues. It is not so much a deliberate evocation of the most difficult of methods, this manner of narration, as a poignant witness to Conrad's own breathless surprise at his discoveries. Mr Henry James, speaking of this enforced collection of oratorical witnesses, says: "It places Mr Conrad absolutely alone as a votary of the way to do a thing that shall make it undergo most doing," and his amazement at Conrad's patient pursuit of unneeded difficulties may seem to us the stranger if we consider that in What Maisie Knew and The Awkward Age he has practised almost precisely the same form himself. Indeed beside the intricate but masterly form of The Awkward Age the duplicate narration of Chance seems child's-play. Mr Henry James makes the mistake of speaking as though Conrad had quite deliberately chosen the form of narration that was most difficult to him, simply for the fun of overcoming the difficulties, the truth being that he has chosen the easiest, the form of narration brought straight from the sea and the ships that he adored, the form of narration used by the Ancient

Mariner and all the seamen before and after him. Conrad must have his direct narrator, because that is the way in which stories in the past had generally come to him. He wishes to deny the effect of that direct and simple honesty that had always seemed so attractive to him. He must have it by word of mouth, because it is by word of mouth that he himself has always demanded it, and if one witness is not enough for the truth of it then must he have two or three.

Consider for a moment the form of three of his most important novels: Lord Jim, Nostromo and Chance. It is possible that Lord Jim was conceived originally as a sketch of character, derived by the author from one scene that was, in all probability, an actual reminiscence. Certainly, when the book is finished, one scene beyond all others remains with the reader; the scene of the inquiry into the loss of the Patna, or rather the vision of Jim and his appalling companions waiting outside for the inquiry to begin. Simply in the contemplation of these four men Conrad has his desired contrast; the skipper of the Patna: "He made me think of a trained baby elephant walking on hind-legs. He was extravagantly gorgeous too— got up in a soiled sleeping-suit, bright green and deep orange vertical stripes, with a pair of ragged straw slippers on his bare feet, and somebody's cast-off pith hat, very dirty and two sizes too small for him, tied up with a manilla rope-yarn on the top of his big head." There are also two other "no-account chaps with him"—a sallow-faced mean little chap with his arm in a sling, and a long individual in a blue flannel coat, as dry as a chip and no stouter than a broomstick, with drooping grey moustaches, who looked about him with an air of jaunty imbecility, and, with these three, Jim, "clean-limbed, clean-faced, firm on his feet, as promising a boy as the sun ever shone on." Here are these four, in the same box, condemned for ever by all right-thinking men. That boy in the same box as those obscene scoundrels! At once the artist has fastened on to his subject, it bristles with active, vital possibilities and discoveries. We, the observers, share the artist's thrill. We watch our author dart upon a subject with the excitement of adventurers discovering a gold mine. How much will it yield? How deep will it go? We are thrilled with the suspense.

Conrad, having discovered his subject, must, for the satisfaction of that honour which is his most deeply cherished virtue, prove to us his authenticity. "I was not there myself," he tells us, "but I can show you someone who was." He introduces us to a first-hand witness, Marlowe or another. "Now tell your story." He has at once the atmosphere in which he is happiest, and so, having his audience clustered about him, unlimited time at everyone's disposal, whiskies and cigars without stint, he lets himself go. He is bothered now by no question but the thorough investigation of his discovery. What had Jim done that he should be in such a case? We must have the story of the loss of the Patna, that marvellous journey across the waters, all the world of the pilgrims, the obscene captain and Jim's fine, chivalrous soul. Marlowe is inexhaustible. He has so much to say and so many fine words in which to say it. At present, so absorbed are we, so successful is he, that we are completely held. The illusion is perfect. We come to the inquiry. One of the judges is Captain Brierley. "What! not know Captain Brierley! Ah! but I must tell you! Most extraordinary thing!"

The world grows around us; a world that can contain the captain of the Patna, Brierley and Jim at the same time! The subject before us seems now so rich that we are expecting to see it burst, at any moment, in the author's hands, but so long as that first visualised scene is the centre of the episode, so long as the experience hovers round that inquiry and the Esplanade outside it, we are held, breathless and believing. We believe even in the eloquent Marlowe. Then the moment passes. Every possible probe into its heart has been made. We are satisfied.

There follows then the sequel, and here at once the weakness of the method is apparent. The author having created his narrator must continue with him. Marlowe is there, untired, eager, waiting to begin again. But the trouble is that we are no longer assured now of the truth and reality of his story. He saw—we cannot for an instant doubt it—that group on the Esplanade; all that he could tell us about that we, breathlessly, awaited. But now we are uncertain whether he is not inventing a romantic sequel. He must go on—that is the truly terrible thing about Marlowe—and at the moment when we question his authenticity we are suspicious of his very existence, ready to be irritated by his flow of words demanding something more authentic than that voice that is now only dimly heard. The author himself perhaps feels this; he duplicates, he even trebles his narrators and with each fresh agent raises a fresh crop of facts, contrasts, habits and histories. That then is the peril of the method. Whilst we believe we are completely held, but let the authenticity waver for a moment and the danger of disaster is more excessive than with any other possible form of narration. Create your authority and we have at once someone at whom we may throw stones if we are not beguiled. Marlowe has certainly been compelled to face, at moments in his career, an angry, irritated audience.

Nostromo is, for the reason that we never lose our confidence in the narrator, a triumphant vindication of these methods. That is not to deny that Nostromo is extremely confused in places, but it is a confusion that arises rather from Conrad's confidence in the reader's fore-knowledge of the facts than in a complication of narrations. The narrations are sometimes complicated—old Captain Mitchell does not always achieve authenticity—but on the whole, the reader may be said to be puzzled, simply because he is told so much about some things and so little about others.

But this assurance of the author's that we must have already learnt the main facts of the case comes from his own convinced sense of the reality of it. This time he has no Marlowe. He was there himself. "Of course," he says to us, "you know all about that revolution in Sulaco, that revolution that the Goulds were mixed up with. Well, I happened to be there myself. I know all the people concerned, and the central figure was not Gould, nor Mitchell, nor Monyngham—no, it was a man about whom no one outside the republic was told a syllable. I knew the man well.... He ..." and there we all are.

The method is, in this case, as I have already said, completely successful. There may be confusions, there may be scenes concerning which we may be expected to be told much and are, in truth, told nothing at all, but these confusions and omissions do, in the end, only add to our conviction of the veracity of it. No one, after a faithful perusal of Nostromo, can possibly doubt of the existence of Sulaco, of the silver mine, of Nostromo and Decoud, of Mrs Gould, Antonio, the Viola girls, of old Viola, Hirsch, Monyngham, Gould, Sotillo, of the death of Viola's wife, of the expedition at night in the painter, of Decoud alone on the Isabels, of Hirsch's torture, of Captain Mitchell's watch—here are characters the most romantic in the world, scenes that would surely, in any other hands, be fantastic melodrama, and both characters and scenes are absolutely supported on the foundation of realistic truth. Not for a moment from the first page to the last do we consciously doubt the author's word.... Here the form of narration is vindicated because it is entirely convincing.

Not so with the third example, Chance. Here, as with Lord Jim, we may find one visualised moment that stands for the whole book and as in the earlier work we look back and see the degraded officers of the Patna waiting with Jim on the Esplanade, so our glance back over Chance reveals to us that moment when the Fynes, from the security of their comfortable home, watch Flora de Barrel flying down the steps of her horrible Brighton house as though the Furies pursued her. That desperate flight is the key of the book. The moment of the chivalrous Captain Anthony's rescue of Flora from a world too villainous for her and too double-faced for him gives the book's theme, and never in all the stories that preceded Flora's has Conrad been so eager to afford us first-hand witnesses. We have, in the first place, the unquenchable Marlowe sitting, with fine phrases at his lips, in a riverside inn. To him enter Powell, who once served with Captain Anthony; to these two add the little Fynes; there surely you have enough to secure your alliance. But it is precisely the number of witnesses that frightens us. Marlowe, unaided, would have been enough for us, more than enough if we are to consider the author himself as a possible narrator. But not only does the number frighten us, it positively hides from us the figures of Captain Anthony and Flora de Barrel. Both the Knight and the Maiden—as the author names them—are retiring souls, and our hearts move in sympathy for them as we contemplate their timid hesitancy before the voluble inquisitions of Marlowe, young Powell and the Fynes. Moreover, the intention of this method that it should secure realistic conviction for the most romantic episodes does not here achieve its purpose, as we have seen that it did in the first half of Lord Jim and the whole of Nostromo. We believe most emphatically in that first narration of young Powell's about his first chance. We believe in the first narration of Marlowe, although quite casually he talks like this: "I do not even think that there was in what he did a conscious and lofty confidence in himself, a particularly pronounced sense of power which leads men so often into impossible or equivocal situations." We believe in the horrible governess (a fiercely drawn figure). We believe in Marlowe's interview with Flora on the pavement outside Anthony's room.

We believe in the whole of the first half of the book, but even here we are conscious that we would prefer to be closer to the whole thing, that it would be pleasant to hear Flora and Anthony speak for themselves, that we resent, a little, Marlowe's intimacy which prevents, with patronising complaisance, the intimacy that we, the readers, might have seemed. Nevertheless we are so far held, we are captured.

But when the second half of the book arrives we can be confident no longer. Here, as in Lord Jim, it is possible to feel that Conrad, having surprised, seized upon, mastered his original moment, did not know how to continue it. The true thing in Lord Jim is the affair of the Patna; the true thing in Chance is Captain Anthony's rescue of Flora after her disaster. But whereas in Lord Jim the sequel to Jim's cowardice has its own fine qualities of beauty and imagination, the sequel to Captain Anthony's rescue of Flora seems to one listener at any rate a pitiably unconvincing climax of huddled melodrama. That chapter in Chance entitled A Moonless Night is, in the first half of it, surely the worst thing that Conrad ever wrote, save only that one early short story, The Return. The conclusion of Chance and certain tales in his volume, Within the Tides, make one wonder whether that alliance between romance and realism that he has hitherto so wonderfully maintained is not breaking down before the baleful strength of the former of these two qualities.

It remains only to be said that when credence so entirely fails, as it must before the end of Chance, the form of narration in Oratio Recta is nothing less than maddening. Suddenly we do not believe in Marlowe, in Powell, in the Fynes: we do not believe even in Anthony and Flora. We are the angrier because earlier in the evening we were so completely taken in. It is as though we had given our money to a deserving cause and discovered a charlatan.

I have described at length the form in which the themes of these books are developed, because it is the form that, here extensively, here quite unobtrusively, clothes all the novels and tales. We are caught and held by the skinny finger of the Ancient Mariner. When he has a true tale to tell us his veritable presence is an added zest to our pleasure. But, if his presence be not true ...

III

If we turn to the themes that engage Joseph Conrad's attention we shall see that in almost every case his subjects are concerned with unequal combats—unequal to his own far-seeing vision, but never to the human souls engaged in them, and it is this consciousness of the blindness that renders men's honesty and heroism of so little account that gives occasion for his irony.

He chooses, in almost every case, the most solid and unimaginative of human beings for his heroes, and it seems that it is these men alone whom he can admire. "If a human soul has vision he simply gives the thing up," we can hear him say. "He can see at once that the odds are too strong for him. But these simple souls, with their consciousness of the job before them and nothing else, with their placid sense of honour and of duty, upon them you may loosen all heaven's bolts and lightnings and they will not quail." They command his pity, his reverence, his tenderness, almost his love. But at the end, with an ironic shrug of his shoulders, he says: "You see. I told you so. He may even think he has won. We know better, you and I."

The theme of Almayer's Folly is a struggle of a weak man against nature, of The Nigger of the Narcissus the struggle of many simple men against the presence of death, of Lord Jim, again, the struggle of a simple man against nature (here the man wins, but only, we feel, at the cost of truth). Nostromo, the conquest of a child of nature by the silver mine which stands over him, conscious of its ultimate victory, from the very first. Chance, the struggle of an absolutely simple and upright soul against the dishonesties of a world that he does not understand. Typhoon, the very epitome of Conrad's themes, is the struggle of McWhirr against the storm (here again it is McWhirr who apparently wins, but we can hear, in the very last line of the book, the storm's confident chuckle of ultimate victory). In Heart of Darkness the victory is to the forest. In The End of the Tether Captain Whalley, one of Conrad's finest figures, is beaten by the very loftiness of his character. The three tales in 'Twixt Land and Sea are all themes of this kind—the struggle of simple, unimaginative men against forces too strong for them. In The Secret Agent Winnie Verloc, another simple character, finds life too much for her and commits suicide. In Under Western Eyes Razumov, the dreamer, is destroyed by a world that laughs at the pains and struggles of insignificant individuals.

Of Conrad's philosophy I must speak in another place: here it is enough to say that it is impossible to imagine him choosing as the character of a story jolly, independent souls who take life for what it gives them and leave defeat or victory to the stars.

Whatever Conrad's books are or are not, it may safely be said that they are never jolly, and his most devoted disciple would, in all probability, resent any suggestion of a lighter hand or a gentler affection. His art, nevertheless, is limited by this persistent brooding over the inequality of life's battle. His humour, often of a very fine kind, is always sinister, because his choice of theme forbids light-heartedness.

Tom Jones and Tristram Shandy would have found Marlowe, Jim and Captain Anthony quite impossibly solemn company—but I do not deny that they might not have been something the better for a little of it.

I have already said that his characters are, for the most part, simple and unimaginative men, but that does not mean that they are so simple that there is nothing in them. The first thing of which one is sure in meeting a number of Conrad's characters is that they have existences and histories entirely independent of their introducer's kind offices. Conrad has met them, has talked to them, has come to know them, but we are sure not only that there is very much more that he could tell us about them if he had time and space, but that even when he had told us all that he knew he would only have touched on the fringe of their real histories.

One of the distinctions between the modern English novel and the mid-Victorian English novel is that modern characters have but little of the robust vitality of their predecessors; the figures in the novel of to-day fade so easily from the page that endeavours to keep them.

In the novels of Mr Henry James we feel at times that the characters fade before the motives attributed to them, in those of Mr Wells before an idea, a curse, or a remedy, in those of Mr Bennett before a creeping wilderness of important insignificances, in those of Mr Galsworthy before the oppression of social inequalities, in those of Mrs Wharton before the shadow of Mr Henry James, even in those of Mr Hardy before the omnipotence of an inevitable God whom, in spite of his inevitability, Mr Hardy himself is arranging in the background; it may be claimed for the characters of Mr Conrad that they yield their solidity to no force, no power, not even to their author's own determination that they are doomed, in the end, to defeat.

This is not for a moment to say that Joseph Conrad is a finer novelist than these others, but this quality he has beyond his contemporaries—namely, the assurance that his characters have their lives and adventures both before and after the especial cases that he is describing to us.

The Russian Tchekov has, in his plays, this gift supremely, so that at the close of The Three Sisters or The Cherry Orchard we are left speculating deeply upon "what happened afterwards" to Gayef or Barbara, to Masha or Epikhadov; with Conrad's sea captains as with Tchekov's Russians we see at once that they are entirely independent of the incidents that we are told about them. This independence springs partly from the author's eager, almost naïve curiosity. It is impossible for him to introduce us to any officer on his ship without whispering to us in an aside details about his life, his wife and family on shore. By so doing he forges an extra link in his chain of circumstantial evidence, but we do not feel that here he is deliberately serving his art—it is only that quality already mentioned, his own astonished delight at the things that he is discovering. We learn, for instance, about Captain McWhirr that he wrote long letters home, beginning always with the words, "My darling Wife," and relating in minute detail each successive trip of the Nan-Shan. Mrs McWhirr, we learn, was "a pretentious person with a scraggy neck and a disdainful manner, admittedly lady-like and in the neighbourhood considered as 'quite superior.' The only secret of her life was her abject terror of the time when her husband would come home to stay for good." Also in Typhoon there is the second mate "who never wrote any letters, did not seem to hope for news from anywhere; and though he had been heard once to mention West Hartlepool, it was with extreme bitterness, and only in connection with the extortionate charges of a boarding-house." How conscious we are of Jim's English country parsonage, of Captain Anthony's loneliness, of Marlowe's isolation. By this simple thread of connection between the land and the ship the whole character stands, human and convincing, before us. Of the sailors on board the Narcissus there is not one about whom, after his landing, we are not curious. There is the skipper, whose wife comes on board, "A real lady, in a black dress and with a parasol."... "Very soon the captain, dressed very smartly and in a white shirt, went with her over the side. We didn't recognise him at all...." And Mr Baker, the chief mate! Is not this little farewell enough to make us his friends for life?

"No one waited for him ashore. Mother died; father and two brothers, Yarmouth fishermen, drowned together on the Dogger Bank; sister married and unfriendly. Quite a lady, married to the leading tailor of a little town, and its leading politician, who did not think his sailor brother-in-law quite respectable enough for him. Quite a lady, quite a lady, he thought, sitting down for a moment's rest on the quarter-hatch. Time enough to go ashore and get a bite, and sup, and a bed somewhere. He didn't like to part with a ship. No one to think about then. The darkness of a misty evening fell, cold and damp, upon the deserted deck; and Mr Baker sat smoking, thinking of all the successive ships to whom through many long years he had given the best of a seaman's care. And never a command in sight. Not once!"

There are others—the abominable Donkin for instance. "Donkin entered. They discussed the account ... Captain Allistoun paid. 'I give you a bad discharge,' he said quietly. Donkin raised his voice: 'I don't want your bloomin' discharge—keep it. I'm goin' ter 'ave a job hashore.' He turned to us. 'No more bloomin' sea for me,' he said, aloud. All looked at him. He had better clothes, had an easy air, appeared more at home than any of us; he stared with assurance, enjoying the effect of his declaration."

In how many novels would Donkin's life have been limited by the part that he was required to play in the adventures of the Narcissus? As it is our interest in his progress has been satisfied by a prologue only. Or there is Charley, the boy of the crew—"As I came up I saw a red-faced, blowzy woman, in a grey shawl, and with dusty, fluffy hair, fall on Charley's neck. It was his mother. She slobbered over him:—'Oh, my boy! my boy!'—'Leggo me,' said Charley, 'leggo, mother!' I was passing him at the time, and over the untidy head of the blubbering woman he gave me a humorous smile and a glance ironic, courageous, and profound, that seemed to put all my knowledge of life to shame. I nodded and passed on, but heard him say again, good-naturedly:—'If you leggo of me this minyt—ye shall 'ave a bob for a drink out of my pay.'"

But one passes from these men of the sea—from McWhirr and Baker, from Lingard and Captain Whalley, from Captain Anthony and Jim, with a suspicion that the author will not convince us quite so readily with his men of the land—and that suspicion is never entirely dismissed. About such men as McWhirr and Baker he can tell us nothing that we will not believe. He has such sympathy and understanding for them that they will, we are assured, deliver up to him their dearest secrets—those little details, McWhirr's wife, Mr Baker's proud sister, Charley's mother, are their dearest secrets. But with the citizens of the other world—with Stein, Decoud, Gould, Verloc, Kazumov, the sinister Nikita, the little Fynes, even the great Nostromo himself—we cannot be so confident, simply because their discoverer cannot yield them that same perfect sympathy.

His theory about these men is that they have, all of them, an idée fixe, that you must search for this patiently, honestly, unsparingly—having found it, the soul of the man is revealed to you. But is it? Is it not possible that Decoud or Verloc, feeling the probing finger, offer up instantly any idée fixe ready to hand because they wish to be left alone? Decoud himself, for instance—Decoud, the imaginative journalist in Nostromo, speculating with his ironic mind upon romantic features, at his heart, apparently cynical and reserved, the burning passion for the beautiful Antonia. He has yielded enough to suggest the truth, but the truth itself eludes us. With Verloc again we have a quite masterly presentation of the man as Conrad sees him. That first description of him is wonderful, both in its reality and its significance. "His eyes were naturally heavy, he had an air of having wallowed, fully dressed, all day on an unmade bed."

With many novelists that would be quite enough, that we should see the character as the author sees him, but because, in these histories, we have the convictions of the extension of the protagonists' lives beyond the stated episodes, it is not enough. Because they have lives independent of the covers of the book we feel that there can be no end to the things that we should be told about them, and they must be true things.

Verloc, for instance, is attached from the first to his idée fixe—namely, that he should be able to retain, at all costs, his phlegmatic state of self-indulgence and should not be jockeyed out of it. At the first sign of threatened change he is terrified to his very soul. Conrad never, for an instant, allows him to leave this ground upon which he has placed him. We see the man tied to his rock of an idée fixe, but he has, nevertheless, we are assured, another life, other motives, other humours, other terrors. It is perhaps a direct tribute to the author's reserve power that we feel, at the book's close, that we should have been told so much more.

Even with the great Nostromo himself we are not satisfied as we are with Captain Whalley or Mr Bates. Nostromo is surely, as a picture, the most romantically satisfying figure in the English novel since Scott, with the single exception of Thackeray's Beatrix—and here I am not forgetting Captain Silver, David Balfour, Catriona, nor, in our own immediate time, young Beauchamp or the hero of that amazing and so unjustly obscure fiction, The Shadow of a Titan. As a picture, Nostromo shines with a flaming colour, shines, as the whole novel shines, with a glow that is flung by the contrasted balance of its romance and realism. From that first vision of him as he rides slowly through the crowds, in his magnificent dress: "... his hat, a gay sombrero with a silver cord and tassels. The bright colours of a Mexican serape twisted on the cantle, the enormous silver buttons on the embroidered leather jacket, the row of tiny silver buttons down the seam of the trousers, the snowy linen, a silk sash with embroidered ends, the silver plates on headstall and saddle ..." to that last moment when—"... in the dimly lit room Nostromo rolled his head slowly on the pillow and opened his eyes, directing at the weird figure perched by his bedside a glance of enigmatic and mocking scorn. Then his head rolled back, his eyelids fell, and the Capatos of the Cargadores died without a word or moan after an hour of immobility, broken by short shudders testifying to the most atrocious sufferings"—we are conscious of his superb figure; and after his death we do, indeed, believe what the last lines of the book assure us—"In that true cry of love and grief that seemed to ring aloud from Punta Mala to Azuera and away to the bright line of the horizon, overhung by a big white cloud shining like a mass of solid silver, the genius of the magnificent Capatuz de Cargadores dominated the dark gulf containing his conquests of treasure and love." His genius dominates, yes—but it is the genius of a magnificent picture standing as a frontispiece to the book of his soul. And that soul is not given us—Nostromo, proud to the last, refuses to surrender it to us. Why is it that the slender sketch of old Singleton in The Nigger of the Narcissus gives us the very heart of the man, so that volumes might tell us more of him indeed, but could not surrender him to us more truly, and all the fine summoning of Nostromo only leaves him beyond our grasp? We believe in Nostromo, but we are told about him—we have not met him.

Nevertheless, at another turn of the road, this criticism must seem the basest ingratitude. When we look back and survey that crowd, so various, so distinct whether it be they who are busied, before our eyes, with the daily life of Sulaco, or the Verloc family (the most poignant scene in the whole of Conrad's art—the drive in the cab of old Mrs Verloc, Winnie and Stevie—compels, additionally, our gratitude) or that strange gathering, the Haldins, Nikita, Laspara, Madame de S—, Peter Ivanovitch, Razumov, at Geneva, or the highly coloured figures in Romance (a book fine in some places, astonishingly second-rate in others), Falk or Amy Foster, Jacobus and his daughter, Jasper and his lover, all these and so many, many more, what can we do but embrace the world that is offered to us, accept it as an axiom of life that, of all these figures, some will be near to us, some more distant? It is, finally, a world that Conrad offers us, not a series of novels in whose pages we find the same two or three figures returning to us—old friends with new faces and new names—but a planet that we know, even as we know the Meredith planet, the Hardy planet, the James planet.

Looking back, we may trace its towns and rivers, its continents and seas, its mean streets and deep valleys, its country houses, its sordid hovels, its vast, untamed forests, its deserts and wildernesses. Although each work, from the vast Nostromo to the minutely perfect Secret Sharer, has its new theme, its form, its separate heart, the swarming life that he has created knows no boundary. And in this, surely, creation has accomplished its noblest work.

CHAPTER III

THE POET

I

 The poet in Conrad is lyrical as well as philosophic. The lyrical side is absent in certain of his works, as, for example, The Secret Agent, and Under Western Eyes, or such short stories as The Informer, or Il Conde, but the philosophic note sounded poetically, as an instrument of music as well as a philosophy, is never absent.

Three elements in the work of Conrad the poet as distinct from Conrad the novelist deserve consideration—style, atmosphere and philosophy. In the matter of style the first point that must strike any constant reader of the novels is the change that is to be marked between the earlier works and the later. Here is a descriptive passage from Conrad's second novel, An Outcast of the Islands:

"He followed her step by step till at last they both stopped, facing each other under the big tree of the enclosure. The solitary exile of the forests great, motionless and solemn in his abandonment, left alone by the life of ages that had been pushed away from him by those pigmies that crept at his foot, towered high and straight above their leader. He seemed to look on, dispassionate and imposing in his lonely greatness, spreading his branches wide in a gesture of lofty protection, as if to hide them in the sombre shelter of innumerable leaves; as if moved by the disdainful compassion of the strong, by the scornful pity of an aged giant, to screen this struggle of two human hearts from the cold scrutiny of glittering stars."

And from his latest novel, Chance:

"The very sea, with short flashes of foam bursting out here and there in the gloomy distances, the unchangeable, safe sea sheltering a man from all passions, except its own anger, seemed queer to the quick glance he threw to windward when the already effaced horizon traced no reassuring limit to the eye. In the expiring diffused twilight, and before the clouded night dropped its mysterious veil, it was the immensity of space made visible—almost palpable. Young Powell felt it. He felt it in the sudden sense of his isolation; the trustworthy, powerful ship of his first acquaintance reduced to a speck, to something almost undistinguishable. The mere support for the soles of his two feet before that unexpected old man becoming so suddenly articulate in a darkening universe."

It must be remembered that the second of these quotations is the voice of Marlowe and that therefore it should, in necessity, be the simpler of the two. Nevertheless, the distinction can very clearly be observed. The first piece of prose is quite definitely lyrical: it has, it cannot be denied, something of the "purple patch." We feel that the prose is too dependent upon sonorous adjectives, that it has the deliberation of work slightly affected by the author's determination that it shall be fine. The rhythm in it, however, is as deliberate as the rhythm of any poem in English, the picture evoked as distinct and clear-cut as though it were, in actual fact, a poem detached from all context and, finally, there is the inevitable philosophical implication to give the argument to the picture. Such passages of descriptive prose may be found again and again in the earlier novels and tales of Conrad, in Almayer's Folly, Tales of Unrest, The Nigger of the Narcissus, Typhoon, Youth, Heart of Darkness, Lord Jim—prose piled high with sonorous and slow-moving adjectives, three adjectives to a noun, prose that sounds like an Eastern invocation to a deity in whom, nevertheless, the suppliant does not believe. At its worst, the strain that its sonority places upon movements and objects of no importance is disastrous. For instance, in the tale called The Return, there is the following passage:—

"He saw her shoulder touch the lintel of the door. She swayed as if dazed. There was less than a second of suspense while they both felt as if poised on the very edge of moral annihilation, ready to fall into some devouring nowhere. Then almost simultaneously he shouted, 'Come back,' and she let go the handle of the door. She turned round in peaceful desperation like one who has deliberately thrown away the last chance of life; and for a moment the room she faced appeared terrible, and dark, and safe—like a grave."

The situation here simply will not bear the weight of the words—"moral annihilation," "devouring nowhere," "peaceful desperation," "last chance of life," "terrible," "like a grave." That he shouted gives a final touch of ludicrous exaggeration to the whole passage.

Often, in the earlier books, Conrad's style has the awkward over-emphasis of a writer who is still acquiring the language that he is using, like a foreigner who shouts to us because he thinks that thus we shall understand him more easily. But there is also, in this earlier style, the marked effect of two influences. One influence is that of the French language and especially of the author of Madame Bovary. When we recollect that Conrad hesitated at the beginning of his career as to whether he would write in French or English, we can understand this French inflection. Flaubert's effect on his style is quite unmistakable. This is a sentence of Flaubert's: "Toutes ses velléités de dénigrement l'envanouissaient sous la poésie du rôle qui l'envahissait; et entraînée vers l'homme par l'illusion du personnage elle tâcha de se figurer sa vie, cette vie retentissante, extraordinaire, splendide ..." and this a sentence of Conrad's: "Her hands slipped slowly off Lingard's shoulders and her arms fell by her side, listless, discouraged, as if to her—to her, the savage, violent and ignorant creature—had been revealed clearly in that moment the tremendous fact of our isolation, of the loneliness, impenetrable and transparent, elusive and everlasting."

Conrad's sentence reads like a direct translation from the French, It is probable, however, that his debt to Flaubert and the French language can be very easily exaggerated, and it does not seem, in any case, to have driven very deeply into the heart of his form. The influence is mainly to be detected in the arrangement of words and sentences as though he had, in the first years of his work, used it as a crutch before he could walk alone.

The second of the early influences upon his style is of far greater importance—the influence of the vast, unfettered elements of nature that he had, for so many years, so directly served. If it were not for his remarkable creative gift that had been, from the very first, at its full strength, his early books would stand as purely lyrical evocations of the sea and the forest. It is the poetry of the Old Testament of which we think in many pages of Almayer's Folly and An Outcast of the Island, a poetry that has the rhythm and metre of a spontaneous emotion. He was never again to catch quite the spirit of that first rapture.

He was under the influence of these powers also in that, at that time, they were too strong for him. We feel with him that he is impotent to express his wonder and praise because he is still so immediately under their sway. His style, in these earlier books, has the repetitions and extended phrases of a man who is marking time before the inspired moment comes to him—often the inspiration does not come because he cannot detach himself with sufficient pause and balance. But in his middle period, in the period of Youth, Typhoon, Heart of Darkness and Nostromo, this lyrical impulse can be seen at its perfection, beating, steadily, spontaneously, with the finest freedom and yet disciplined, as it were, by its own will and desire. Compare, for a moment, this passage from Typhoon with that earlier one from The Outcast of the Islands that I quoted above:

"He watched her, battered and solitary, labouring heavily in a wild scene of mountainous black waters lit by the gleam of distant worlds. She moved slowly, breathing into the still core of the hurricane the excess of her strength in a white cloud of steam, and the deep-toned vibration of the escape was like the defiant trumpeting of a living creature of the sea impatient for the renewal of the contest. It ceased suddenly. The still air moaned. Above Jakes' head a few stars shone into the pit of black vapours. The inky edge of the cloud-disc frowned upon the ship under the patch of glittering sky. The stars too seemed to look at her intently, as if for the last time, and the cluster of their splendour sat like a diadem on a lowering brow."

That is poet's work, and poet's work at its finest. Instead of impressing us, as the earlier piece of prose, with the fact that the author has made the very most of a rather thin moment—feels, indeed, himself that it is thin—we are here under the influence of something that can have no limits to the splendours that it contains. The work is thick, as though it had been wrought by the finest workman out of the heart of the finest material—and yet it remains, through all its discipline, spontaneous.

These three tales, Typhoon, Youth and Heart of Darkness, stand by themselves as the final expression of Conrad's lyrical gift. We may remember such characters as McWhirr, Kurtz, Marlowe, but they are figures as the old seneschal in The Eve of St Agnes or the Ancient Mariner himself are figures. They are as surely complete poems, wrought and finished in the true spirit of poetry, as Whitman's When Lilac first on the Door-yard bloomed or Keats' Nightingale. Their author was never again to succeed so completely in combining the free spirit of his enthusiasm with the disciplined restraint of the true artist.

The third period of his style shows him cool and clear-headed as to the things that he intends to do. He is now the slightly ironic artist whose business is to get things on to paper in the clearest possible way. He is conscious that in the past he has been at the mercy of sonorous and high-sounding adjectives. He will use them still, but only to show them that they are at his mercy. Marlowe, his appointed minister, is older—he must look back now on the colours of Youth with an indulgent smile. And when Marlowe is absent, in such novels as The Secret Agent and Under Western Eyes, in such a volume of stories as A Set of Six, the lyrical beat in the style is utterly abandoned—we are led forward by sentences as grave, as assured, and sometimes as ponderous as a city policeman. Nevertheless, in that passage from Chance quoted at the beginning of the chapter, although we may be far from the undisciplined enthusiasm of An Outcast of the Islands, the lyrical impulse still remains. Yes, it is there, but—"Young Powell felt it." In that magical storm that was Typhoon God alone can share our terror and demand our courage; in the later experience young Powell is our companion.

The question of style devolves here directly into the question of atmosphere. There may roughly be said to be four classes of novelists in the matter of atmosphere. There is the novelist who, intent upon his daily bread or game of golf, has no desire to be worried by such a perplexing business. He produces stories that might without loss play the whole of their action in the waiting-room of an English railway station. There is the novelist who thinks that atmosphere matters immensely, who works hard to produce it and does produce it in thick slabs. There are the novelists whose theme, characters and background react so admirably that the atmosphere is provided simply by that reaction—and there, finally, it is left, put into no relation with other atmospheres, serving no further purpose than the immediate one of stating the facts. Of this school are the realists and, in our own day, Mr Arnold Bennett's Brighton background in Hilda Lessways or Mrs Wharton's New York background in The House of Mirth offer most successful examples of such realistic work. The fourth class provides us with the novelists who wish to place their atmosphere in relation with the rest of life. Our imagination is awakened, insensibly, by the contemplation of some scene and is thence extended to the whole vista of life, from birth to death; although the scene may actually be as remote or as confined as space can make it, its potential limits are boundless, its progression is extended beyond all possibilities of definition. Such a moment is the death of Bazarov in Fathers and Children, the searching of Dmitri in The Brothers Karamazov, the scene at the theatre in The Ring and the Book, the London meeting between Beauchamp and René in Beauchamp's Career. It is not only that these scenes are "done" to the full extent of their "doing," it is also that they have behind them the lyrical impulse that unites them with all the emotion and beauty in the history of the world; Turgéniev, Dostoievsky, Browning, Meredith were amongst the greatest of the poets. Conrad, at his highest moments, is also of that company.

But it is not enough to say that this potential atmosphere is simply lyrical. Mr Chesterton, in his breathless Victorian Age in Literature, has named this element Glamour.

In writing of the novels by George Eliot he says: "Indeed there is almost every element of literature, except a certain indescribable thing called Glamour, which was the whole stock-in-trade of the Brontës, which we feel in Dickens when Quilp clambers amid rotten wood by the desolate river; and even in Thackeray, when Edmond wanders like some swarthy crow about the dismal avenues of Castlewood." Now this matter of Glamour is not all, because Dickens, for instance, is not at all potential. His pictures of Quilp or the house of the Dedlocks or Jonas Chuzzlewit's escape after the murder do not put us into touch with other worlds—but we may say, at any rate, that when, in a novel atmosphere is potential, it is certain also to have glamour.

The potential qualities of Conrad's atmosphere are amongst his very strongest gifts and, if we investigate the matter, we see that it is his union of Romance and Realism that gives such results. Of almost no important scene in his novels is it possible to define the boundaries. In The Outcast of the Islands, when Willems is exiled by Captain Lingard, the terror of that forest has at its heart not only the actual terror of that immediate scene, minutely and realistically described—it has also the terror of all our knowledge of loneliness, desolation, the power of something stronger than ourselves. In Lord Jim the contrast of Jim with the officers of the Patna is a contrast not only immediately vital and realised to the very fringe of the captain's gay and soiled pyjamas, but also potential to the very limits of our ultimate conception of the eternal contrast between good and evil, degradation and vigour, ugliness and beauty. In The Nigger of the Narcissus the death of the negro, James Wait, immediately affects the lives of a number of very ordinary human beings whose friends and intimates we have become—but that shadow that traps the feet of the negro, that alarms the souls of Donkin, of Belfast, of Singleton, of the boy Charlie, creeps also to our sides and envelops for us far more than that single voyage of the Narcissus.

When Winnie Verloc, her old mother and the boy Stevie take their journey in the cab it does not seem ludicrous to us that the tears of "that large female in a dark, dusty wig, and ancient silk dress festooned with dingy white cotton lace" should move us as though Mrs Verloc were our nearest friend. That mournful but courageous journey remains in our mind as an intimate companion of our own mournful and courageous experiences. Such examples might be multiplied quite indefinitely.

He has always secured his atmosphere by his own eager curiosity about significant detail, but his detail is significant, not because he wishes to impress his reader with the realism of his picture, but rather because he is, like a very small boy in a strange house, pursuing the most romantic adventures for his own pleasure and excitement only. We may hear, with many novelists, the click of satisfaction with which they drive another nail into the framework that supports their picture. "Now see how firmly it stands," they say. "That last nail settled it." But Conrad is utterly unconscious as to his readers' later credulity—he is too completely held by his own amazing discoveries. Sometimes, as in The Return, when no vision is granted to him, it is as though he were banging on a brass tray with all his strength so that no one should perceive his own grievous disappointment at his failure. But, in his real discoveries, how the atmosphere piles itself up, around and about him, how we follow at his heels, penetrating the darkness, trusting to his courage, finding ourselves suddenly blinded by the blaze of Aladdin's cave! If he is tracing the tragedy of Willems and Almayer, a tragedy that has for its natural background the gorgeous, heavy splendour of those unending forests, he sees details that belong to the austerest and most sharply disciplined realism. We see Lakamba, asleep under the moon, slapping himself in his dreams to keep off the mosquitoes; a bluebottle comes buzzing into the verandah above the dirty plates of a half-finished meal and defies Lingard and Almayer, so that they are like men disheartened by some tremendous failure; the cards with which Lingard tries to build a house for Almayer's baby are "a dirty double pack" with which he used to play Chinese bézique—it bored Almayer but the old seaman delighted in it, considering it a remarkable product of Chinese genius. The atmosphere of the terrible final chapters is set against this picture of a room in which Mrs Willems is waiting for her abominable husband:

"Bits of white stuff; rags yellow, pink, blue; rags limp, brilliant and soiled, trailed on the floor, lay on the desk amongst the sombre covers of books soiled, greasy, but stiff-backed in virtue, perhaps, of their European origin. The biggest set of bookshelves was partly hidden by a petticoat, the waistband of which was caught upon the back of a slender book pulled a little out of the row so as to make an improvised clothes-peg. The folding canvas bedstead stood anyhow, parallel to no wall, as if it had been, in the process of transportation to some remote place, dropped casually there by tired bearers. And on the tumbled blankets that lay in a disordered heap on its edge, Joanna sat.... Through the half-open shutter a ray of sunlight, a ray merciless and crude, came into the room, beat in the early morning upon the safe in the far-off corner, then, travelling against the sun, cut at midday the big desk in two with its solid and clean-edged brilliance; with its hot brilliance in which a swarm of flies hovered in dancing flight over some dirty plate forgotten there amongst yellow papers for many a day!"

And this room is set in the very heart of the forests—"the forests unattainable, enigmatical, for ever beyond reach like the stars of heaven—and as indifferent." Had I space I could multiply from every novel and tale examples of this creation of atmosphere by the juxtaposition of the lyrical and the realistic—the lyrical pulse beating through realistic detail and transforming it. I will, however, select one book, a supreme example of this effect. What I say about Nostromo may be proved from any other work of Conrad's.

The theme of Nostromo is the domination of the silver of the Sulaco mine over the bodies and souls of the human beings who live near it. The light of the silver shines over the book. It is typified by "the white head of Higuerota rising majestically upon the blue." Conrad, then, in choosing his theme, has selected the most romantic possible, the spirit of silver treasure luring men on desperately to adventure and to death. His atmosphere, therefore, is, in its highest lights, romantic, even until that last vision of all of "the bright line of the horizon, overhung by a big white cloud shining like a mass of solid silver." Sulaco burns with colour. We can see, as though we had been there yesterday, those streets with the coaches, "great family arks swayed on high leathern springs full of pretty powdered faces in which the eyes looked intensely alive and black," the houses, "in the early sunshine, delicate primrose, pale pink, pale blue," or, after dark, from Mrs Gould's balcony "towards the plaza end of the street the glowing coals in the hazeros of the market women cooking their evening meal glowed red along the edge of the pavement. A man appeared without a sound in the light of a street lamp, showing the coloured inverted triangle of his broidered poncho, square on his shoulders, hanging to a point below his knees. From the harbour end of the Calle a horseman walked his soft-stepping mount, gleaming silver-grey abreast each lamp under the dark shape of the rider." Later there is that sinister glimpse of the plaza, "where a patrol of cavalry rode round and round without penetrating into the streets which resounded with shouts and the strumming of guitars issuing from the open doors of pulperias ... and above the roofs, next to the perpendicular lines of the cathedral towers the snowy curve of Higuerota blocked a large space of darkening blue sky before the windows of the Intendencia." In its final created beauty Sulaco is as romantic, as coloured as one of those cloud-topped, many-towered towns under whose gates we watch Grimm's princes and princesses passing—but the detail of it is built with careful realism demanded by the "architecture of Manchester or Birmingham." We wonder, as Sulaco grows familiar to us, as we realise its cathedral, its squares and streets and houses, its slums, its wharves, its sea, its hills and forests, why it is that other novelists have not created towns for us.

Anthony Trollope did, indeed, give us Barchester, but Barchester is a shadow beside Sulaco. Mr Thomas Hardy's Wessex map is the most fascinating document in modern fiction, with the possible exception of Stevenson's chart in Treasure Island. Conrad, without any map at all, gives us a familiarity with a small town on the South American coast that far excels our knowledge of Barsetshire, Wessex and John Silver's treasure. If any attentive reader of Nostromo were put down in Sulaco tomorrow he would feel as though he had returned to his native town. The detail that provides this final picture is throughout the book incessant but never intruding. We do not look back, when the novel is finished, to any especial moment of explanation or introduction. We have been led, quite unconsciously, forward. We are led, at moments of the deepest drama, through rooms and passages that are only remembered, many hours later, in retrospect. There is, for instance, the Aristocratic Club, that "extended to strangers the large hospitality of the cool, big rooms of its historic quarters in the front part of a house, once a residence of a high official of the Holy Office. The two wings, shut up, crumbled behind the nailed doors, and what may be described as a grove of young orange-trees grown in the unpaved patio concealed the utter ruin of the back part facing the gate. You turned in from the street, as if entering a secluded orchard, where you came upon the foot of a disjointed staircase, guarded by a moss-stained effigy of some saintly bishop, mitred and staffed, and bearing the indignity of a broken nose meekly, with his fine stone hands crossed on his breast. The chocolate-coloured faces of servants with mops of black hair peeped at you from above; the click of billiard balls came to your ears, and, ascending the steps, you would perhaps see in the first sala, very stiff upon a straight-backed chair, in a good light, Don Pépé moving his long moustaches as he spelt his way, at arm's-length, through an old Sta Marta newspaper. His horse—a strong-hearted but persevering black brute, with a hammer head—you would have seen in the street dozing motionless under an immense saddle, with its nose almost touching the curbstone of the sidewalk!"

How perfectly recollected is that passage! Can we not hear the exclamation of some reader: "Yes—those orange-trees! It was just like that when I was there!" How convinced we are of Conrad's unimpeachable veracity! How like him are those remembered details, "the nailed doors," "the fine stone hands," "at arm's-length"!—and can we not sniff something of the author's impatience to let himself go and tell us more about that "hammer-headed horse" of whose adventures with Don Pépé he must remember enough to fill a volume!

He is able, therefore, upon this foundation of a minute and scrupulous realism to build as fantastic a building as he pleases without fear of denying Truth. He does not, in Nostromo at any rate, choose to be fantastic, but he is romantic, and our final impression of the silver mine and the town under its white shining shadow is of something both as real and as beautiful as any vision of Keats or Shelley. But with the colour we remember also the grim tragedy of the life that has been shown to us. Near to the cathedral and the little tinkering streets of the guitars were the last awful struggles of the unhappy Hirsch. We remember Nostromo riding, with his silver buttons, catching the red flower flung to him out of the crowd, but we remember also his death and the agony of his defeated pride. Sotillo, the vainest and most sordid of bandits, is no figure for a fairy story.

Here, then, is the secret of Conrad's atmosphere. He is the poet, working through realism, to the poetic vision of life. That intention is at the heart of his work from the first line of Almayer's Folly to the last line of Victory. Nostromo is not simply the history of certain lives that were concerned in a South American revolution. It is that history, but it is also a vision, a statement of beauty that has no country, nor period, and sets no barrier of immediate history or fable for its interpretation....

When, however, we come finally to the philosophy that lies behind this creation of character and atmosphere we perceive, beyond question, certain limitations.

III

 As we have already seen, Conrad is of the firm and resolute conviction that life is too strong, too clever and too remorseless for the sons of men.

It is as though, from some high window, looking down, he were able to watch some shore, from whose security men were for ever launching little cockle-shell boats upon a limitless and angry sea. He observes them, as they advance with confidence, with determination, each with his own sure ambition of nailing victory to his mast; he alone can see that the horizon is limitless; he can see farther than they—from his height he can follow their fortunes, their brave struggles, their fortitude to the very last. He admires that courage, the simplicity of that faith, but his irony springs from his knowledge of the inevitable end.

There are, we may thankfully maintain, other possible views of life, and it is, surely, Conrad's harshest limitation that he should never be free from this certain obsession of the vanity of human struggle. So bound is he by this that he is driven to choose characters who will prove his faith. We can remember many fine and courageous characters of his creation, we can remember no single one who is not foredoomed to defeat. Jim wins, indeed, his victory, but at the close: "And that's the end. He passes away under a cloud, inscrutable at heart, forgotten, unforgiven, and excessively romantic.... He goes away from a living woman to celebrate his pitiless wedding with a shadowy ideal of conduct."

Conrad's ironical smile that has watched with tenderness the history of Jim's endeavours, proclaims, at the last, that that pursuit has been vain—as vain as Stein's butterflies.

And, for the rest, as Mr Curle in his study of Conrad has admirably observed, every character is faced with the enemy for whom he is, by character, least fitted. Nostromo, whose heart's desire it is that his merits should be acclaimed before men, is devoured by the one dragon to whom human achievements are nothing—lust of treasure.

McWhirr, the most unimaginative of men, is opposed by the most tremendous of God's splendid terrors and, although he saves his ship from the storm, so blind is he to the meaning of the things that he has witnessed that he might as well have never been born. Captain Brierley, watching the degradation of a fellow-creature from a security that nothing, it seems, can threaten, is himself caught by that very degradation.... The Beast in the Jungle is waiting ever ready to leap—the victim is always in his power.

It comes from this philosophy of life that the qualities in the human soul that Conrad most definitely admires are blind courage and obedience to duty. His men of brain—Marlowe, Decoud, Stein—are melancholy and ironic: "If you see far enough you must see how hopeless the struggle is." The only way to be honestly happy is to have no imagination and, because Conrad is tender at heart and would have his characters happy, if possible, he chooses men without imagination. Those are the men of the sea whom he has known and loved. The men of the land see farther than the men of the sea and must, therefore, be either fools or knaves. Towards Captain Anthony, towards Captain Lingard he extends his love and pity. For Verloc, for Ossipon, for old De Barral he has a disgust that is beyond words. For the Fynes and their brethren he has contempt. For two women of the land, Winnie Verloc and Mrs Gould, he reserves his love, and for them alone, but they have, in their hearts, the simplicity, the honesty of his own sea captains.

This then is quite simply his philosophy. It has no variation or relief. He will not permit his characters to escape, he will not himself try to draw the soul of a man who is stronger than Fate. His ironic melancholy does not, for an instant, hamper his interest—that is as keen and acute as is the absorption of any collector of specimens—but at the end of it all, as with his own Stein: "He says of him that he is 'preparing to leave all this: preparing to leave ...' while he waves his hand sadly at his butterflies."

Utterly opposed is it from the philosophy of the one English writer whom, in all other ways, Conrad most obviously resembles—Robert Browning. As philosophers they have no possible ground of communication, save in the honesty that is common to both of them. As artists, both in their subjects and their treatment of their subjects, they are, in many ways, of an amazing resemblance, although the thorough investigation of that resemblance would need far more space than I can give it here. Browning's interest in life was derived, on the novelist's side of him, from his absorption in the affairs, spiritual and physical, of men and women; on the poet's side, in the question again spiritual and physical, that arose from those affairs. Conrad has not Browning's clear-eyed realisation of the necessity of discovering the individual philosophy that belongs to every individual case—he is too immediately enveloped in his one overwhelming melancholy analysis. But he has exactly that eager, passionate pursuit of romance, a romance to be seized only through the most accurate and honest realism.

Browning's realism was born of his excitement at the number and interest of his discoveries; he chose, for instance, in Sordello the most romantic of subjects, and, having made his choice, found that there was such a world of realistic detail in the case that, in his excitement, he forgot that the rest of the world did not know quite as much as he did. Is not this exactly what we may say of Nostromo? Mr Chesterton has written of Browning: "He substituted the street with the green blind for the faded garden of Watteau, and the 'blue spirt of a lighted match' for the monotony of the evening star." Conrad has substituted for the lover serenading his mistress' window the passion of a middle-aged, faded woman for her idiot boy, or the elopement of the daughter of a fraudulent speculator with an elderly, taciturn sea captain.

The characters upon whom Robert Browning lavished his affection are precisely Conrad's characters. Is not Waring Conrad's man?

And for the rest, is not Mr Sludge own brother to Verloc and old De Barrel? Bishop Blougram first cousin to the great Personage in The Secret Agent, Captain Anthony brother to Caponsacchi, Mrs Gould sister to Pompilia? It is not only that Browning and Conrad both investigate these characters with the same determination to extract the last word of truth from the matter, not grimly, but with a thrilling beat of the heart, it is also that the worlds of these two poets are the same. How deeply would Nostromo, Decoud, Gould, Monyngham, the Verlocs, Flora de Barrel, McWhirr, Jim have interested Browning! Surely Conrad has witnessed the revelation of Caliban, of Childe Roland, of James Lee's wife, of the figures in the Arezzo tragedy, even of that bishop who ordered his tomb at St Praxed's Church, with a strange wonder as though he himself had assisted at these discoveries!

Finally, The Ring and the Book, with its multiplied witnesses, its statement as a "case" of life, its pursuit of beauty through truth, the simplicity of the characters of Pompilia, Caponsacchi and the Pope, the last frantic appeal of Guido, the detail, encrusted thick in the walls of that superb building—here we can see the highest pinnacle of that temple that has Chance, Lord Jim, Nostromo amongst its other turrets, buttresses and towers.

Conrad is his own master—he has imitated no one, he has created, as I have already said, his own planet, but the heights to which Browning carried Romantic-Realism showed the author of Almayer's Folly the signs of the road that he was to follow.

If, as has often been said, Browning was as truly novelist as poet, may we not now say with equal justice that Conrad is as truly poet as novelist?

CHAPTER IV

ROMANCE AND REALISM

I

The terms, Romance and Realism, have been used of late years very largely as a means of escape from this business of the creation of character. The purely romantic novel may now be said to be, in England at any rate, absolutely dead. Mr Frank Swinnerton, in his study of Robert Louis Stevenson, said: "Stevenson, reviving the never-very-prosperous romance of England, created a school which has brought romance to be the sweepings of an old costume-chest;... if romance is to be conventional in a double sense, if it spring not from a personal vision of life, but is only a tedious virtuosity, a pretence, a conscious toy, romance as an art is dead. The art was jaded when Reade finished his vociferous carpet-beating; but it was not dead. And if it is dead, Stevenson killed it!"

We may differ very considerably from Mr Swinnerton with regard to his estimate of Stevenson's present and future literary value without denying that the date of the publication of St Ives was also the date of the death of the purely romantic novel.

But, surely, here, as Mr Swinnerton himself infers, the term "Romantic" is used in the limited and truncated idea that has formed, lately the popular idea of Romance. In exactly the same way the term "Realism" has, recently, been most foolishly and uncritically handicapped. Romance, in its modern use, covers everything that is removed from reality: "I like romances," we hear the modern reader say, "because they take me away from real life, which I desire to forget." In the same way Realism is defined by its enemies as a photographic enumeration of unimportant facts by an observant pessimist. "I like realism," admirers of a certain order of novel exclaim, "because it is so like life. It tells me just what I myself see every day—I know where I am."

Nevertheless, impatient though we may be of these utterly false ideas of Romance and Realism, a definition of those terms that will satisfy everyone is almost impossible. I cannot hope to achieve so exclusive an ambition—I can only say that to myself Realism is the study of life with all the rational faculties of observation, reason and reminiscence—Romance is the study of life with the faculties of imagination. I do not mean that Realism may not be emotional, poetic, even lyrical, but it is based always upon truth perceived and recorded—it is the essence of observation. In the same way Romance may be, indeed must be, accurate and defined in its own world, but its spirit is the spirit of imagination, working often upon observation and sometimes simply upon inspiration. It is, at any rate, understood here that the word Romance does not, for a moment, imply a necessary divorce from reality, nor does Realism imply a detailed and dusty preference for morbid and unagreeable subjects. It is possible for Romance to be as honestly and clearly perceptive as Realism, but it is not so easy for it to be so because imagination is more difficult of discipline than observation. It is possible for Realism to be as eloquent and potential as Romance, although it cannot so easily achieve eloquence because of its fear of deserting truth. Moreover, with regard to the influence of foreign literature upon the English novel, it may be suggested that the influence of the French novel, which was at its strongest between the years of 1885 and 1895, was towards Realism, and that the influence of the Russian novel, which has certainly been very strongly marked in England during the last years, is all towards Romantic-Realism. If we wished to know exactly what is meant by Romantic-Realism, such a novel as The Brothers Karamazov, such a play as The Cherry Orchard are there before us, as the best possible examples. We might say, in a word, that Karamazov has, in the England of 1915, taken the place that was occupied, in 1890, by Madame Bovary....

II

It is Joseph Conrad whose influence is chiefly responsible for this development in the English novel. Just as, in the early nineties, Mr Henry James and Mr Rudyard Kipling, the one potential, the other kinetic, influenced, beyond all contemporary novelists, the minds of their younger generation, so to-day, twenty-five years later, do Mr Joseph Conrad and Mr H. G. Wells, the one potential, the other kinetic, hold that same position.

Joseph Conrad, from the very first, influenced though he was by the French novel, showed that Realism alone was not enough for him. That is to say that, in presenting the case of Almayer, it was not enough for him merely to state as truthfully as possible the facts. Those facts, sordid as they are, make the story of Almayer's degradation sufficiently realistic, when it is merely recorded and perceived by any observer. But upon these recorded facts Conrad's imagination, without for a moment deserting the truth, worked, beautifying, ennobling it, giving it pity and terror, above all putting it into relation with the whole universe, the whole history of the cycle of life and death.

As I have said, the Romantic novel, in its simplest form, was used, very often, by writers who wished to escape from the business of the creation of character. It had not been used for that purpose by Sir Walter Scott, who was, indeed, the first English Romantic-Realist, but it was so used by his successors, who found a little optimism, a little adventure, a little colour and a little tradition go a long way towards covering the required ground.

Conrad had, from the first, a poet's—that is to say, a romantic—mind, and his determination to use that romance realistically was simply his determination to justify the full play of his romantic mind in the eyes of all honest men.

In that intention he has absolutely succeeded; he has not abated one jot of his romance—Nostromo, Lord Jim, Heart of Darkness are amongst the most romantic things in all our literature—but the last charge that any critic can make against him is falsification, whether of facts, of inference or of consequences.

The whole history of his development has for its key-stone this determination to save his romance by his reality, to extend his reality by his romance. He found in English fiction little that could assist him in this development; the Russian novelists were to supply him with his clue. This whole question of Russian influence is difficult to define, but that Conrad has been influenced by Turgéniev a little and by Dostoievsky very considerably, cannot be denied. Crime and Punishment, The Idiot, The Possessed, The Brothers Karamazov are romantic realism at the most astonishing heights that this development of the novel is ever likely to attain. We will never see again heroes of the Prince Myshkin, Dmitri Karamazov, Nicolas Stavrogin build, men so real to us that no change of time or place, age or sickness can take them from us, men so beautifully lit with the romantic passion of Dostoievsky's love of humanity that they seem to warm the whole world, as we know it, with the fire of their charity. That power of creating figures typical as well as individual has been denied to Conrad. Captain Anthony, Nostromo, Jim do not belong to the whole world, nor do they escape the limitations and confinements that their presentation as "cases" involves on them. Moreover, Conrad does not love humanity. He feels pity, tenderness, admiration, but love, except for certain of his sea heroes, never, and even with his sea heroes it is love built on his scorn of the land. Dostoievsky scorned no one and nothing; as relentless in his pursuit of the truth as Stendhal or Flaubert, he found humanity, as he investigated it, beautiful because of its humanity—Conrad finds humanity pitiable because of its humanity.

Nevertheless he has been influenced by the Russian writer continuously and sometimes obviously. In at least one novel, Under Western Eyes, the influence has led to imitation. For that reason, perhaps, that novel is the least vital of all his books, and we feel as though Dostoievsky had given him Razumov to see what he could make of him, and had remained too overwhelmingly curious an onlooker to allow independent creation. What, however, Conrad has in common with the creator of Raskolnikov is his thrilling pursuit of the lives, the hearts, the minutest details of his characters. Conrad alone of all English novelists shares this zest with the great Russian. Dostoievsky found his romance in his love of his fellow-beings, Conrad finds his in his love of beauty, his poet's cry for colour, but their realism they find together in the hearts of men—and they find it not as Flaubert, that they make of it a perfect work of art, not as Turgéniev, that they may extract from it a flower of poignant beauty, not as Tolstoi, that they may, from it, found a gospel—simply they pursue their quest because the breathless interest of the pursuit is stronger than they. They have, both of them, created characters simply because characters demanded to be created. We feel that Emma Bovary was dragged, painfully, arduously, against all the strength of her determination, out of the shades where she was lurking. Myshkin, the Karamazovs, and, in their own degree, Nostromo, Almayer, McWhirr, demanded that they should be flung upon the page.

Instead of seizing upon Romance as a means of avoiding character, he has triumphantly forced it to aid him in the creation of the lives that, through him, demand existence. This may be said to be the great thing that Conrad has done for the English novel—he has brought the zest of creation back into it; the French novelists used life to perfect their art—the Russian novelists used art to liberate their passion for life. That at this moment in Russia the novel has lost that zest, that the work of Kouprin, Artzybashev, Sologub, Merejkovsky, Andreiev, shows exhaustion and sterility means nothing; the stream will soon run full again. Meanwhile we, in England, know once more what it is to feel, in the novel, the power behind the novelist, to be ourselves in the grip of a force that is not afraid of romance nor ashamed of realism, that cares for life as life and not as a means of proving the necessity for form, the danger of too many adjectives, the virtues of the divorce laws or the paradise of free love.

III

Finally, what will be the effect of the work of Joseph Conrad upon the English novel of the future? Does this Romantic-Realism that he has provided for us show any signs of influencing that future? I think that it does. In the work of all of the more interesting younger English novelists—in the work of Mr E. M. Forster, Mr D. H. Lawrence, Mr J. D. Beresford, Mr W. L. George, Mr Frank Swinnerton, Mr Gilbert Cannan, Miss Viola Meynell, Mr Brett Young—this influence is to be detected. Even with such avowed realists as Mr Beresford, Mr George and Mr Swinnerton the realism is of a nature very different from the realism of even ten years ago, as can be seen at once by comparing so recent a novel as Mr Swinnerton's On the Staircase with Mr Arnold Bennett's Sacred and Profane Love, or Mr Galsworthy's Man of Property—and Mr E. M. Forster is a romantic-realist of most curious originality, whose Longest Journey and Howard's End may possibly provide the historian of English literature with dates as important as the publication of Almayer's Folly in 1895. The answer to this question does not properly belong to this essay.

It is, at any rate, certain that neither the old romance nor the old realism can return. We have been shown in Nostromo something that has the colour of Treasure Island and the reality of New Grub Street. If, on the one hand, the pessimists lament that the English novel is dead, that everything that can be done has been done, there is, surely, on the other hand, some justification for the optimists who believe that at few periods in English literature has the novel shown more signs of a thrilling and original future.

For signs of the possible development of Conrad himself one may glance for a moment at his last novel, Victory.

The conclusion of Chance and the last volume of short stories had shown that there was some danger lest romance should divorce him, ultimately, from reality. Victory, splendid tale though it is, does not entirely reassure us. The theme of the book is the pursuit of almost helpless uprightness and innocence by almost helpless evil and malignancy; that is to say that the strength and virtue of Heyst and Lena are as elemental and independent of human will and effort as the villainy and slime of Mr Jones and Ricardo. Conrad has here then returned to his old early demonstration that nature is too strong for man and I feel as though, in this book, he had intended the whole affair to be blown, finally, sky-high by some natural volcanic eruption. He prepares for that eruption and when, for some reason or another, that elemental catastrophe is prevented he consoles himself by strewing the beach of his island with the battered corpses of his characters. It is in such a wanton conclusion, following as it does immediately upon the finest, strongest and most beautiful thing in the whole of Conrad—the last conversation between Heyst and Lena—that we see this above-mentioned divorce from reality. We see it again in the more fantastic characteristics of Mr Jones and Ricardo, in the presence of the Orang-Outang, and in other smaller and less important effects. At the same time his realism, when he pleases, as in the arrival of the boat of the thirst-maddened trio on the island beach, is as magnificent in its austerity and truth as ever it was.

Will he allow his imagination to carry him wildly into fantasy and incredibility? He has not, during these last years, exerted the discipline and restraint that were once his law.

Nevertheless, at the last, when one looks back over twenty years, from the Almayer's Folly of 1895 to the Victory of 1915, one realises that it was, for the English novel, no mean nor insignificant fortune that brought the author of those books to our shores to give a fresh impetus to the progress of our literature and to enrich our lives with a new world of character and high adventure.

Hugh Walpole – A Short Biography

Sir Hugh Seymour Walpole, CBE was born in Auckland, New Zealand, on March 13th, 1884.

His parents had moved to New Zealand in 1877, but his mother, Mildred, unable to settle there, eventually persuaded, in 1889, her husband, Somerset, an Anglican clergyman, to accept another post, this time in New York.

Walpole's early years involved being educated by a Governess until, in 1893, his parents decided he needed an English education and the young Walpole was sent to England.

He first attended a preparatory school in Truro. He naturally missed his family but was reasonably happy. A move to Sir William Borlase's Grammar School in Marlow in 1895, found him bullied, frightened and miserable. He later said, "The food was inadequate, the morality was 'twisted', and Terror—sheer, stark unblinking Terror—stared down every one of its passages ... The excessive desire to be loved that has always played so enormous a part in my life was bred largely, I think, from the neglect I suffered there".

In 1896 Somerset Walpole, hearing of his son's unhappiness, moved him to the King's School, Canterbury. For two years he settled but was undistinguished as a pupil. The following year, 1897, Walpole senior was appointed principal of Bede College, Durham, and his son was moved again; to be a day boy for four years at Durham School. Day boys were regarded as the underclass by boarders, and Bede College was the subject of snobbery within the university. His sense of isolation increased. He continually took refuge in the local library, where he read all the novels of Austen, Fielding, Scott and Dickens and many others. He was voracious in reading.

Walpole wrote in 1924: "I grew up ... discontented, ugly, abnormally sensitive, and excessively conceited. No one liked me—not masters, boys, friends of the family, nor relations who came to stay; and I do not in the least wonder at it. I was untidy, uncleanly, excessively gauche. I believed that I was profoundly misunderstood, that people took my pale and pimpled countenance for the mirror of my soul, that I had marvellous things of interest in me that would one day be discovered".

From 1903 to 1906 Walpole studied history at Emmanuel College, Cambridge and there, in 1905, had his first work published, the critical essay "Two Meredithian Heroes". Here he met and fell under the spell of A C Benson. Walpole's religious beliefs, previously sacrosanct, were fading, and Benson helped him through that personal crisis. Walpole was also attempting to cope with his homosexual feelings, which, for a while, focused on Benson.

Benson gently declined Walpole's advances. They remained friends, but Walpole, feeling rebuffed, gradually downgraded the relationship. Two years later Benson's diary entry on Walpole's subsequent social career reveals his thoughts on his protégé's progress: "He seems to have conquered Gosse completely. He spends his Sundays in long walks with H G Wells. He dines every week with Max Beerbohm and R Ross ... and this has befallen a not very clever young man of 23. Am I a little jealous?— no, I don't think so. But I am a little bewildered ... I do not see any sign of intellectual power or perception or grasp or subtlety in his work or himself. ... I should call him curiously unperceptive. He does not, for instance, see what may vex or hurt or annoy people. I think he is rather tactless—though he is himself very sensitive. The strong points about him are his curiosity, his vitality, his eagerness, and the emotional fervour of his affections. But he seems to me in no way likely to be great as an artist.

Somerset Walpole, himself the son of an Anglican priest, hoped that his eldest son would follow him into the ministry. Walpole was concerned for his father's feelings. So much so that on graduation from Cambridge in 1906 he took a post as a lay missioner at the Mersey Mission to Seamen in Liverpool. He described that as one of the "greatest failures of my life". Walpole resigned after six months.

From April to July 1907 Walpole was in Germany, privately tutoring children before returning, in 1908, to teach French at Epsom College.

Walpole now found the desire to fully immerse himself in the literary world. He moved to London to become a book reviewer for The Standard and to write fiction in his spare time. He had by this time come to terms with his homosexuality. His encounters were discreet, as they were illegal in Britain. He was constantly searching for "the perfect friend".

In 1909, Walpole published his first novel, The Wooden Horse, the story of a staid, snobbish English family shaken by the return of one of their own from a more out-going New Zealand. The book received good reviews but sold little.

Better was to come in 1911 when he published Mr Perrin and Mr Traill. The Guardian observed that "the setting of Mr Perrin and Mr Traill was clearly drawn from life". The boys of Epsom College were delighted with the thinly disguised version of their school, but the authorities were not, and Walpole was persona non grata there for many years. It was an early illustration of his capacity, noted by Benson, for unthinkingly giving offence, though being hypersensitive to criticism himself.

In early 1914 Henry James wrote an article for The Times Literary Supplement surveying the younger generation of British novelists and comparing them with their eminent elders. In the latter category James put Bennett, Conrad, Galsworthy, Hewlett and H G Wells. The four new authors were Walpole, Gilbert Cannan, Compton Mackenzie and D H Lawrence. From Walpole's point of view one of the greatest living authors had publicly ranked him among the finest young British novelists.

As war approached, Walpole realised that his poor eyesight would disqualify him from serving in the armed forces. He volunteered for the police, but was turned down. He then accepted an appointment, based in Moscow, reporting for The Saturday Review and The Daily Mail. Although he was allowed to visit the front in Poland, these dispatches were not enough to stop hostile comments at home that he was not doing his bit for the war effort.

Walpole was ready with a counter; an appointment as a Russian officer, in the Sanitar. He explained they were "part of the Red Cross that does the rough work at the front, carrying men out of the trenches, helping at the base hospitals in every sort of way, doing every kind of rough job. They are an absolutely official body and I shall be one of the few Englishmen in the world wearing Russian uniform".

While training Walpole spent many hours gaining fluency in Russian, and writing a literary biography of Joseph Conrad.

In the summer of 1915 he worked on the Austrian-Russian front, assisting at operations in field hospitals and retrieving the dead and wounded from the battlefield. Writing home to Arnold Bennett he said "A battle is an amazing mixture of hell and a family picnic—not as frightening as the dentist, but absorbing, sometimes thrilling like football, sometimes dull like church, and sometimes simply physically sickening like bad fish. Burying the dead afterwards is worst of all."

During a skirmish in June 1915 Walpole rescued a wounded soldier; his Russian comrades refused to help and this meant Walpole had to carry one end of a stretcher, dragging the man to safety. He was awarded the Cross of Saint George.

In October 1915 he returned to England to visit family and friends and to stay at a cottage he had purchased in Cornwall. In January 1916 he was asked by the Foreign Office to return to Petrograd.

Before going his novel, The Dark Forest, was published. It drew on his experiences in Russia, and was more sombre than much of his earlier fiction. Reviews were highly favourable; The Daily Telegraph commented on "a high level of imaginative vision ... reveals capacity and powers in the author which we had hardly suspected before."

Back in Petrograd his diary entry for March 13th records "Thirty two today! Should have been a happy day but was completely clouded for me by reading in the papers of Henry James' death. This was a terrible shock to me."

By late 1917 it was clear to Walpole and the authorities that his work was at an end. On November 7th he left, missing the Bolshevik Revolution, which began that very day.

In London Walpole was appointed to a post at the Foreign Office and remained there until resigning in February 1919. For his wartime work he was awarded the CBE in 1918.

Walpole continued to write and publish and now also began a career on the highly lucrative lecture tour in the United States.

He made his first lecture tour in 1919, receiving an enthusiastic welcome wherever he went. It was noted that Walpole's "genial and attractive appearance, his complete lack of aloofness, his exciting fluency as a speaker and his obvious and genuine liking for his hosts" combined to win him a large American following. The success of his talks led to an increase in lecturing fees, greater sales of his books, and large sums from American publishers keen to print his latest fiction.

A keen music lover, Walpole, in 1920, heard a new tenor at the Proms, impressed he sought him out. Lauritz Melchior became one of the most important friendships of his life, and Walpole did much to foster the singer's budding career. Wagner's son Siegfried engaged Melchior for the Bayreuth Festival in 1924 and succeeding years. Walpole attended, and met Adolf Hitler, then recently released from prison after an attempted putsch.

In 1924 Walpole moved to a house, Brackenburn, near Keswick in the Lake District. His large income enabled him to maintain his London flat in Piccadilly, but Brackenburn was his main home for the rest of his life.

At the end of 1924 Walpole met Harold Cheevers, who soon became his friend and companion and remained so for the rest of his life. Cheevers, a policeman, with a wife and two children, left the police force and entered Walpole's service as his chauffeur. Walpole trusted him completely, and gave him extensive control over his affairs. Whether Walpole was at Brackenburn or Piccadilly, Cheevers was almost always with him, and often accompanied him on overseas trips. Walpole provided a house in Hampstead for Cheevers and his family.

During the mid-twenties Walpole produced two of his best-known novels in the macabre vein that he drew on from time to time, exploring the fascination of fear and cruelty. The Old Ladies (1924) is a study of a timid elderly spinster exploited and eventually frightened to death by a predatory widow. Portrait of a Man with Red Hair (1925) depicts the malign influence of a manipulative, insane father on his family and others.

Walpole continued a series of stories for children, begun in 1919 with Jeremy, taking the young hero's story forward with Jeremy and Hamlet (the boy's dog) in 1923, and Jeremy at Crale in 1927.

In 1930 Walpole wrote possibly his best-known work, Rogue Herries, a historical novel set in the Lake District. The Daily Mail considered it "not only a profound study of human character, but a subtle and intimate biography of a place." He followed it with four sequels and an almost finished fifth.

Hollywood, in the shape of MGM, invited him in 1934 to write the script for a film of David Copperfield. Walpole enjoyed life in Hollywood, but as one who rarely revised any of his work he found it a bore to produce sixth and seventh drafts at the behest of the studio. He also had a small acting role in the film; he played the Vicar of Blunderstone delivering a boring sermon that sends David to sleep.

Walpole's performance was a success. The sermon was improvised and the producer, David O Selznick, had mischievously called for retake after retake to try to make him dry up, but Walpole fluently delivered a different extempore address each time.

The critical and commercial success of the film led to a return in 1936. Arriving, he found the studio had no idea which films they wanted him to work on, and he had eight weeks of highly paid leisure, during which he wrote a short story and worked on a novel. He was eventually asked to write the script for Little Lord Fauntleroy. He spent most of his fees on paintings; he was an avid collector and left many to the Tate in London on his death. His last lecture tour, also in 1936, was primarily to raise funds to pay US taxes which he had neglected to pay earlier.

In 1937 Walpole was offered a knighthood. He accepted although Kipling, Hardy, Galsworthy had all refused. "I'm not of their class... Besides I shall like being a knight," he said.

Walpole's taste for adventure did not diminish in his last years. In 1939 he was commissioned to report for William Randolph Hearst's newspapers on the funeral in Rome of Pope Pius XI, the conclave to elect his successor, and the subsequent coronation. In the weeks between the funeral and Pius XII's election Walpole, with his customary fluency, wrote much of Roman Fountain, a mixture of fact and fiction about the city. It was his last overseas visit.

After the outbreak of the Second World War Walpole remained in England, dividing his time between London and Keswick, where he continued to write with his usual speed. He completed a fifth novel in the Herries series and began work on a sixth.

Unfortunately his health was undermined by diabetes. He overexerted himself at the opening of Keswick's fund-raising "War Weapons Week" in May 1941, making a speech after taking part in a lengthy march.

Sir Hugh Seymour Walpole, CBE died of a heart attack at Brackenburn, aged 57 on June 1st, 1941. He was buried in St John's churchyard in Keswick.

Hugh Walpole – A Concise Bibliography

Books
The Wooden Horse (1909)
Maradick at Forty: A Transition (1910)
Mr Perrin and Mr Traill (1911) (Revised for the US version as The Gods and Mr Perrin)
The Prelude to Adventure (1912)
Fortitude (1913)
The Duchess of Wrexe, Her Decline and Death (1914)
The Golden Scarecrow (Short Stories) (1915)
Prologue
Hugh Seymour
Henry Fitzgeorge Strether
Ernest Henry
Angelina
Bim Rochester
Nancy Ross
'Enery

Barbara Flint
Sarah Trefusis
Young John Scarlet
Epilogue
The Dark Forest (1916)
Joseph Conrad (1916)
The Green Mirror (1918)
The Secret City (1919)
Jeremy (1919)
The Art of James Branch Cabell (1920)
The Captives (1920)
The Thirteen Travellers (Short Stories) (1920)
Absalom Jay
Fanny Close
The Hon Clive Torby
Miss Morganhurst
Peter Westcott
Lucy Moon
Mrs Porter and Miss Allen
Lois Drake
Mr Nix
Lizzie Rand
Nobody
Bombastes Furioso
The Young Enchanted (1921)
The Cathedral (1922)
Jeremy and Hamlet (1923)
The Crystal Box (1924) Privately published by Walpole – limited edition of 150 copies
The Old Ladies (1924)
The English Novel: Some Notes on its Evolution (1924)
Portrait of a Man with Red Hair (1925)
Harmer John (1926)
Reading: An Essay (1926)
Jeremy at Crale (1927)
Anthony Trollope (1928)
My Religious Experience (1928)
The Silver Thorn (Short Stories) (1928)
The Little Donkeys with the Crimson Saddles
The Tiger
No Unkindness Intended
Ecstasy
A Picture
Old Elizabeth (A Portrait)
The Etching
Chinese Horses
The Tarn
Major Wilbraham
A Silly Old Fool

The Enemy
The Enemy in Ambush
The Dove
Bachelors
Wintersmoon (1928)
Farthing Hall (1929) With J B Priestley
Hans Frost (1929)
Rogue Herries (1930)
Above the Dark Circus (1931) Published in the US as Above the Dark Tumult
Judith Paris (1931)
The Apple Trees: Four Reminiscences (1932) Limited edition of 500 copies
The Fortress (1932)
A Letter to a Modern Novelist (1932)
All Souls' Night (Short Stories) 1933
The Whistle
The Silver Mask
The Staircase
A Carnation for an Old Man
Tarnhelm – or The Death of my Uncle Robert
Mr Oddy
Seashore Macabre – A Moment's Experience
Lilac
The Oldest Talland
The Little Ghost
Mrs Lunt
Sentimental but True
Portrait in Shadow
The Snow
The Ruby Glass
Spanish Dusk
Vanessa (1933)
Extracts from a Diary (1934) Privately published by Walpole
Captain Nicholas (1934)
Cathedral Carol Service (1934) An episode from "The Inquisitor"
The Inquisitor (1935)
Claude Houghton: Appreciations (1935) With Clemence Dane
A Prayer for My Son (1936)
John Cornelius: His Life and Adventures (1937)
Head in Green Bronze and Other Stories(1938)
Head in Green Bronze
The German
The Exile
The Train
The Haircut
Let The Bores Tremble
The Honey-Box
The Fear of Death
The Field with Five Trees

Having No Hearts
The Conjurer
The Joyful Delaneys (1938)
The Sea Tower (1939)
Roman Fountain (1940)
The Bright Pavilions (1940)
The Blind Man's House (1941)
Open Letter of an Optimist (1941)
The Killer and the Slain (1942)
Katherine Christian (1943)
Mr Huffam and Other Stories (1948)
The White Cat
The Train to the Sea
The Perfect Close
Service for the Blind
The Faithful Servant
Miss Thom
Women are Motherly
The Beard
The Last Trump
Green Tie
The Church in the Snow
Mr Huffam – A Christmas Story

Short Stories
The following stories appeared in the Windsor Magazine

The Dog and the Dragon In Reminiscence (October 1923)
Red Amber (December 1923)
The Garrulous Diplomatist (December 1924)
The Adventure of Mrs Farbman (January 1925)
The Adventure of the Imaginative Child (February 1925)
The Happy Optimist (March 1925)
The Dyspeptic Critic (April 1925)
The Man Who Lost His Identity (May 1925)
The Adventure of the Beautiful Things (June 1925)
The War Babies are Growing Up! (November 1934)

Plays
The Young Huntress (1933)
The Cathedral (adaptation of his 1922 novel) (1936)
The Haxtons (1939)

Editor
In 1932 Walpole edited The Waverley Pageant: Best Passages from the Novels of Sir Walter Scott. In 1937 he edited a compilation of short stories, A Second Century of Creepy Stories (Hutchinson, 1937), by

a range of writers including Guy de Maupassant, M. R. James, Henry James, Walter de la Mare, Oliver Onions, Walpole himself ("Tarnhelm") and twenty-one others.

www.ingramcontent.com/pod-product-compliance
Lightning Source LLC
Chambersburg PA
CBHW072234190626
46809CB00017B/2000